Clash

a novel

Other books in the Soul Surfer Series:

a novel

By Rick Bundschuh
Inspired by Bethany Hamilton

ZONDERKIDZ

Clash
Copyright © 2007 by Bethany Hamilton
Illustrations © 2007 by Taia Morley

Requests for information should be addressed to:

Zonderkidz, 3900 *Sparks Dr., Grand Rapids, Michigan 49546*

This Edition: 978-0-310-74582-2

Library of Congress Cataloging-in-Publication Data

Bundschuh, Rick, 1951-
    Clash / by Rick Bundschuh; inspired by Bethany Hamilton. p. cm. -- (Soul Surfer series)
    Summary: One year after losing an arm in a shark attack, fourteen-year-old Bethany Hamilton is still a champion surfer and serves as an inspiration to others, but her faith is tested when an unpleasant new girl seeks her friendship.
    ISBN-13: 978-0-310-71222-0
    1. Hamilton, Bethany — Juvenile fiction. [1. Hamilton, Bethany — Fiction. 2. Surfing — Fiction. 3. Christian life — Fiction. 4. Amputees — Fiction. 5. People with disabilities — Fiction. 6. Samoa — Fiction.] I. Title.
PZ7.B915126Cla 2007
[Fic]--dc22
                                                    2006029322

Cover design: Cindy Davis
Interior design: Christine Orejuela-Winkelman

For Allegra

Introduction

There is something you need to know—this book is fiction. The story and most of the people in it are made up.

Except for Bethany.

I have known Bethany Hamilton since she was a little kid. I have shot paintballs at her brothers, spent lots of time with her parents, Tom and Cheri, and surfed with them all. My role in their lives has been that of a friend and pastor. I was at the hospital the day Bethany was attacked by the shark and have helped Bethany get her fascinating story told.

So when I tell you a story about Bethany, her friends, or her parents, please understand that I am writing about what I am pretty sure they would really do and say if they found themselves in the situations described in this book.

And I am not really writing fiction when I tell you that Bethany is a smoothie addict or that she has a dog named Ginger or that she is homeschooled so she can train for surf contests. A lot of that stuff is exactly how Bethany is and how she lives her life.

You will probably see that I don't try to pretend that Bethany is a saint or some kind of perfect human being. I have seen her get in very hot water for camp pranks taken too far, and I know that from time to time she can be as cranky, self-absorbed, or annoying as any of us. The picture I will paint of her is that of a normal young lady, who, although imperfect, tries her best to love and honor God and let him guide her steps.

This is the Bethany that I know.

I will tell you something about Hawaii too. You see, I live there and surf all the same spots as Bethany and know many of the same characters that populate the island. The places, cultural quirks, and names are pretty much exactly what you would find if you came to visit or live here.

Because surfing is a big part of what Bethany does, I will try to explain to those of you who have never experienced the sport what it is like to ride the warm, clear waves of Hawaii. I can do this with some confidence because I was surfing long before Bethany was even born. But please understand that describing surfing to someone who has never surfed is like trying to describe the taste of a mango to someone who has never sunk their teeth into that rich orange fruit. Words can only get you so far.

Finally, these stories are not just about tanned, talented surf kids in an exotic land. They are about situations that people everywhere can relate to. Even here in paradise there are problems, and when you take a good look at them, you find that those same problems are found in Tulsa, Tucson, or Timbuktu!

So, I hope you enjoy this little adventure.

Rick Bundschuh
Kauai, Hawaii

Prologue

"Bethany!" The voice sounded small and far away as the salty ocean breeze blew across her face. Bethany grinned and turned back to enjoy the view. She loved how the morning sun ricocheted off the ocean surface, sending jewels of light across the tops of the waves. From underneath the huge ironwood trees, she had an awesome view of the northern coastline with its soaring jade-colored cliffs and sandy beaches.

She could experience this a million times over and never grow tired of it.

She was a child of the ocean.

We all are, Bethany thought, looking up to see her friends jogging toward her through the warm sand with their boards.

"Let's go!" she said, running for the water. Then, without another word, she plunged into the Pacific, her red-and-white surfboard floating under her.

Beneath the water, Bethany blew bubbles and opened her eyes. She could see the reef spreading out, with little alleys of sand running between the dark green reef heads. She finally broke the surface and whipped her long, white-blonde hair back while stroking hard and deep in the water with both arms. Her laughter echoed over the water as she chased her friends through the shallow reef and out into deeper water.

This was Bethany's Hawaii—beautiful sun-drenched islands, the water lapping around her as both hands gripped the nose of her board.

Bethany glanced down at the watch around her left wrist. It was especially designed for girl surfers—it was waterproof, dainty yet rugged, and included a tide function. She caught the time—8:07 a.m.—and then let her arm slide off into the water while continuing to hold the nose of the board with her right hand.

Suddenly, something gray and large loomed up, startling the breath out of her. She thrashed and twisted away from it.

Then the bright sky turned dark. The water, the green hills, her friends, and even her surfboard dissolved into deep gray and then black...

Bethany gasped and lurched up in bed.

Blinking rapidly in the dark room, she could feel her heart pounding in her chest. *Just a dream,* she reminded herself as she listened to the soft breathing of her friend Malia coming from the futon on the floor.

Just a dream... Despite knowing that, Bethany reached over and felt for her left arm. The place where it should have been was hollow and empty, and she felt a momentary stab of grief over her loss.

Not just a dream—a *nightmare!* It was a nightmare that had replayed what had actually happened to her just a year ago when she'd been attacked by a shark—a horrible day that had cost Bethany her arm and almost took her life.

At least the nightmares didn't come as often anymore. Not like they used to.

Bethany felt the beat of her heart slowly return to normal as the memory of the horrible attack faded. In the darkness of her room, the lanky teenager stretched out under the sheets and let the comfort and safety of her own bed, in the house she had lived in all her life, with a family who loved her, erase the nightmare.

I'm still alive, she thought. *Still breathing. Still laughing. Still surfing.* Everyone told her it was a miracle...and she knew that. Deep down she also sensed there was a reason behind the miracle—even if she didn't know what the reason was...yet.

With a sigh, she sank back into her soft pillow and let sleep envelop her once again.

By morning she would have no recollection of the nightmare that once again had startled her out of a deep sleep. Nor would she remember waking at all that night.

She was a child of the ocean—but she was also a child of God. And as with all of his children, he came and comforted her. The comfort came in the form of love from her family and friends. They helped her deal with the bad dreams and soothed her with words that washed over her like a gentle ocean tide.

A couple of miles away, another girl lay awake in her bed, eyes wide open as she stared up at the ceiling and wondered if anyone would ever understand how lonely she was—or how rotten she felt inside.

Out of nowhere came a high-pitched buzz.

The noise, centered in her left ear, sounded as if a dentist had mistakenly gone to work on her eardrum. Only it wasn't a dentist.

It was a mosquito.

The thirteen-year-old gave an angry swat at her ear, and the sound disappeared. She sat straight up in bed.

The black, star-speckled sky peeked in from between Jenna's bedroom curtains as she fanned herself with her hand. It was so *hot*—a sticky, humid hot that was nothing like the dry heat of her home in Arizona.

Jenna squirmed to get comfortable in this new bed, in this new home, thousands of miles and a whole ocean away from everything and everyone she had ever known.

The glowing face of the clock on the bedside table read 2:02 a.m. It was still too early for the ever-present roosters to start their song.

Then the itching started—on her feet, between her fingers, on her legs, arms, and face. The mosquito buzzing in her ear had only been one of an army of bloodsucking intruders that had somehow found their way into Jenna's house and honed in on her sleeping form by sensing the carbon dioxide from her exhaled breath. In the blackness, Jenna muttered words of exasperation as she scratched wildly at the itching bites.

Here she was in paradise—Kauai, the crown jewel of the Hawaiian Islands—or so she was told. She preferred to think of it as jail. She had been dragged halfway around the world because her mother "needed a change" (which was code for "I met a man") and then plunked down in this mosquito-infested cell of a room.

Why am I even here? she wondered, even though she knew there was no one to give her an answer.

She missed Arizona. She missed the vast stretches of desert that were the entranceway to her home, the snow-crested mountains, the thick forests that smelled richly of pine. Most of all, she missed her horse, Patchwork.

Well, not *her* horse, exactly. Jenna owned a share of the horse, a share that her mother had bought for Jenna's eleventh birthday. On Saturdays after she had finished with her chores, Jenna would ride her bike the two miles to the stables. The rest of the afternoon would be spent caring for Patchwork and riding through the woods on the sturdy mare. Jenna had probably stomped in protest and shed more tears over the horse than she did over anything else when they left Arizona.

As silly as it seemed, she even missed her old bed, her dresser, the well-worn but comfortable sofa, and the nicked kitchen table where she had dyed Easter eggs, frosted Christmas cookies with friends, and completed her homework.

They were all gone, sold in a massive garage sale because her mother said they weren't worth the expense of shipping them all the way to Hawaii.

Jenna squirmed, sweating and itching in the small rented house filled with bloodthirsty mosquitoes, croaking geckos, and giant cockroaches. It was jail all right. Soon she would be forced to start school with total strangers, whose everyday use of pidgin English was mumbo-jumbo to her, and where she, with her freckles, white skin, and red hair, would stand out like a sore thumb.

It didn't matter that this place was a land of endless summer weather. It didn't matter that you could pick coconuts off the ground or ripe mangos and avocados off the trees. It didn't matter that the rain was warm, the sunsets incredible, or the ocean enticing. She didn't belong here. This was not her home.

She was only here because her mother "needed a change."

Jenna buried her face in her pillow and wept loudly, consumed by an overpowering wave of loneliness and frustration, wishing with all of her heart that someone would comfort her.

one

Dawn crept over the jagged green mountains, and the sunlight slid into the bedroom window of fourteen-year-old Bethany Hamilton.

Bethany groaned, pulling the sheets up over her head as the light bounced off the polished surface of the trophies and mementos that lined her walls.

Her room, like her spirit, reflected the ocean.

Small bottles of shells, collected season after season, sat on the shelf. The size and beauty of them showed progress from a toddler, scooping up tiny treasures from the sand, to a young girl with mask and snorkel, snatching up larger, rarer specimens from their home on the reef, and finally, to a world traveler, bringing home exotic shells from beaches all around the world.

Her CDs, stacked willy-nilly on the shelf and spilling onto the floor, had titles that showed a taste for not only surf-saturated sounds but also for Christian rock.

On a hook near the door hung a selection of bathing suits, each different in color and style but all bearing the logo of *Rip Curl*, the surf clothing manufacturer that long ago had spotted the girl's talent and made sure that she had plenty of their product to wear as she surfed.

"Come on, Bethany," a voice, still full of sleep, mumbled from near the floor. "I hear the surf calling us."

"We stayed up way too late last night," Bethany's muffled voice protested from under the sheets.

"There wasn't any school to get up for this morning."

"I never have to get up for school in the morning," Bethany said.

There was a short pause, and then the voice on the floor replied, "That's because you're a home-school geek!"

Bethany dropped the sheets and grinned. "Malia, you're just jealous because you have to climb on that sweaty ol' schoolbus that I drive by on my way to surf every morning."

Suddenly, the room exploded with a flurry of flying pillows as the two girls batted at one another and squealed in mock pain and laughter.

In the midst of the battle, the door burst open and Ginger, Bethany's Shar-Pei dog, flew into the fray, barking and jumping up and down. Both girls laughed even harder.

Breathing hard, the pillow fight soon calmed down. Moments later, Bethany's mom, Cheri, popped her head around the corner.

"It's about time you sleepyheads woke up. I've had breakfast ready for a while now—thought you two would be on dawn patrol."

"Malia made me stay up and watch *Master and Commander* again. She's in love with one of the lieutenants."

"I'm sure she had to force you," said Cheri Hamilton with a twinkle in her eye. "Malia, how was the futon?"

"Awesome! But Mrs. Hamilton—did you know Bethany *snores*?"

"I do not!" protested Bethany.

"You do too!" Malia grinned.

With that, the pillow war started up again.

"Come on, girls, breakfast is waiting. If you don't hurry, Tim will eat it all," Mrs. Hamilton said. "And don't forget to turn off the fans. Our electric bills are high enough as it is."

"Sure, Mom," Bethany said in between swats with a pillow.

Within a few minutes, the girls emerged from the bedroom, giggling: Bethany, tall and lanky with a snarled tangle of sun-bleached hair, and Malia, small and thin-boned, with thick black hair and oval-shaped eyes that gave hint to an Asian background. Two normal girls. The only thing that would attract the attention of a stranger would be the empty left sleeve of Bethany's T-shirt.

It was still strange how in one moment in time—one blink of an eye—her life had changed forever. The fourteen-foot shark that attacked her had quickly severed her left arm, taking a massive bite out of her board before he swam off, leaving her to die. But God had other plans for Bethany.

Bleeding severely from the traumatic wound, a quarter-mile offshore and forty-five minutes from the nearest hospital, Bethany had been blessed by the quick work and calm heads of the Blanchard family—Alana, Byron, and their dad Holt—who "just happened" to be there at the moment she needed someone to save her life.

Soon after that came the media firestorm, and Bethany's close scrape with death was splashed over every television station and newspaper. But it was her remarkable spirit, coupled with a genuine faith in God, that kept her in the media spotlight, not as a tragic story but as a model of determination and courage.

Within a month of the attack, Bethany overcame her fears and surfed again. Not only did she relearn the art of surfing, but she went on to win contests.

Bethany's mom made allowances for her daughter's handicap: oranges and bananas were peeled and the bread was cut before the girls came to the table. But for Bethany, the loss of an arm provided only a temporary challenge for most things and a change of activity or choices for other ones.

Tying shoelaces with one hand was difficult and time-consuming. Bethany had already spent most of her life barefoot or wearing inexpensive rubber sandals, but now any shoes or boots she would need to purchase had to be put through the "can-I-do-this-with-one-hand?" test. Slip-ons worked best. Velcro straps performed the job as well.

Tackling simple tasks such as peeling a giant jabon—a grapefruit-type fruit that grows all over Hawaii—was performed by sitting on the floor, holding the fruit between her bare feet, and tearing into the thick skin with her right hand.

For surfing, Bethany had made one compensation: a handle attached to the deck of the surfboard gave her a head start to get to her feet. By losing an arm, she'd lost the ability to use the push-up grasp surfers use to hang onto the surfboard when diving deep enough to get under the crushing water of a broken wave.

The girls had finished their breakfast by the time Bethany's older brother Tim, the second in the line of three siblings, came stumbling from his room.

"Bethany," Tim said groggily, "you didn't leave any for me!"

"Snooze, you lose," Bethany shot back.

"There's more on the counter." Their mother grinned, shaking her head. "Juice is in the fridge."

"Oh, and Tim," Bethany added playfully, "last one up has to do dishes. Bye!"

And with that, the girls giggled and darted from the table. "We're ready to go, Mom!"

ot until you put away the futon and straighten your room," Mom said, evoking a grin from Tim.

Within minutes, the chores were done and Bethany and Malia were in the garage, pulling their surfboards from their resting places against the wall.

"Whatcha think, Bethany?" Malia said. "The Bay? Pine Trees? Chicken Wings? Rock Quarry?"

"I'm not sure," Bethany said, chewing her bottom lip. "I didn't check the surf report this morning, but I bet my mom did."

"I wish my mom and dad surfed," Malia said.

Bethany grinned. "Noah says we were all born with saltwater in our veins."

Malia laughed. "Sounds like something your brother would say."

"North, northeast swell—four to six feet," Mrs. Hamilton announced as she came around the corner. "My bet is on Kalihiwai, especially with the tide at this hour."

Both girls grinned at each other.

"Let's go! I *love* that wave, and it's one of the best barrels on the island," Bethany said excitedly. Then she noticed her friend's hesitation. "You okay with that, Malia?"

"Sure," Malia said, trying to sound more confident than she felt.

Bethany sensed her friend's uneasiness and reached for Malia's hand.

"Malia, you can do it! Even though you're a goofy foot like me and this is a big right, you still have an advantage. At least you can grab your rail with your left hand. I gotta pull in real tight to make it, so we'll both be working at it."

Malia brightened at the encouragement.

It was fun surfing with Bethany. She always made it fun. It wasn't about who was better, bigger, braver, stronger, or more fluid. It was mostly about having fun and enjoying what God had provided: the warm sun, the crystal-clear water, the turtles darting along the cliffs, and the crisp tubing waves.

"Don't forget, girls," Mrs. Hamilton cheerfully reminded them, "the best surfer in the water isn't the one who's ripping the hardest, it's the one who's having the most fun!"

Both girls looked at each other and then back to Bethany's mom. "Ancient surf wisdom," she added gravely, and they all laughed.

With that, Mrs. Hamilton slid behind the wheel of her minivan packed with surfboards, and the two girls piled into the van, followed by Ginger.

"Hope you don't mind if I stop by the bank on the way," Cheri said as she backed out of the driveway and saw Bethany's frown in the rearview mirror.

"Mom! The bank isn't even *open* this early," Bethany said impatiently, wanting to get to the beach.

"The ATM is always open, Bethany," Cheri said—and Bethany saw her *mom's* frown in the rearview mirror. Not good. Cheri opened her mouth to say something else, but Malia beat her to the punch...with something that sounded like a *growl*.

"What—" Cheri started.

"Sorry, Mom!" Bethany said, suddenly contrite, and then she and Malia grinned at each other, pleased with their new code.

"Okay...so what was the growl for?"

"Aslan," Malia announced, as if that would explain everything. Both girls laughed, seeing Mrs. Hamilton's confused expression.

"We were talking about the *Chronicles of Narnia* books last night," Bethany explained. "I told Malia it would be cool if God could roar at us like Aslan to let us know if we did something wrong—"

"So, I offered to roar at Bethany if she does something wrong," Malia added. "And she offered to roar at me if I do something wrong."

"Ah," Cheri said, "that sounds like the mark of a true friendship!"

Bethany nodded, glancing shyly at Malia as her mom pulled into the shopping center. She *was* a true friend—even if it didn't bother her to hit the waves late as much as it did Bethany. She watched her mom head for the ATM, while Malia scrambled across the lot to get some lip balm.

"Take your time," Bethany called after Malia with a mischievous grin. "We're only missing perfect waves!" She tilted her car seat back as far as it would go and leaned back so the warm sun and soft trade winds could blow across her face. All she needed now was her board and a wave.

That's when she heard the fight.

"You don't care!" a girl's voice shouted in the clear morning air.

"I do care," an older woman's voice replied. Not quite as loudly, but clearly perturbed.

"If you *really* cared about me, you would've never done it. You would've never made me move here!"

Bethany felt an uncomfortable feeling wash over her, and she sank lower in her seat. She didn't want to hear what was going on, but it was hard not to. *Way too loud to block it out, that's for sure.*

"You don't care if I'm happy! All you care about is if *he's* happy!" yelled the girl.

Mother/daughter feud, no doubt about it.

"Look, life has been stressful for me too," the mother shot back. "I'm doing the best I can to satisfy everyone, but you—you're never satisfied!"

The young voice rose another octave.

"Oh, sure! You were thinking about my feelings the whole time. Like you cared that I had to leave my horse, like you cared that I had to leave my friends, like you cared that you made us sell everything to come here! You're nothing more than a self-centered..." And then she used a swear word on her mother. In fact, she unleashed a torrent of horrible words on her mother.

Bethany winced.

The Hamilton kids had always been taught to respect and honor their parents—even if they disagreed with them. And while Bethany knew that from time to time she could get a little sarcastic— like this morning with the diversion to the bank before going surfing—to truly show disrespect at the level that was coming from the car nearby was unthinkable.

It was a firm family rule.

The voices in the other car scrambled together as the mother returned the verbal abuse, and the argument ended with both parties yelling and swearing at each other at the top of their lungs.

Bethany considered for a moment showing herself by sliding up into her seat when, suddenly, they stopped shouting. A car started, and Bethany raised her head slowly to catch a glimpse at the brawlers.

She only managed to catch the back end of an older-model tan sedan with a broken taillight speeding away.

"Unbelievable!" Bethany muttered.

A few moments later, her mom appeared at the car door. "Okay! Let's go surfing!"

"Malia isn't back yet," said Bethany with a distracted frown.

Then the slap of flip-flops could be heard as Malia ran to the car.

"Sorry, sorry!" she said. "I got behind a guy who paid for all his stuff with change."

"Excuses, excuses," Bethany said teasingly, then turned back to her mom. "Mom, what would you do if Noah, Tim, or I ever swore at you?"

"First, I would cry," said her mother.

"Cry?"

"I'd cry because I would be hurt by your lack of respect."

"Oh," Bethany said softly with a side glance at Malia, but her best friend was turned, looking out the window.

"And then I would tell your father," said Cheri. "And then *you* would cry." Bethany's mother smiled.

"Ah!" Bethany said. "Then it would be Ivory soap time."

"A full diet of Ivory soap, followed by restriction to your room until you're eighteen, and hours of slave labor—oh, and surfboards hacked to pieces."

"You mean you wouldn't pull off my fingernails too?" Bethany laughed.

"Honestly, I don't know what your father would do," her mother said. "But I'm sure it would cure the situation once and for all. Why? Are you thinking of cussing me out?"

"No, I just overheard some girl cursing at her mom, and it kinda made me sick to my stomach. I just don't get families that do stuff like that." She glanced at Malia, who appeared to be thinking hard about all that was being said.

"We've taught you well, thank God. It *should* bother you. Who was it? Someone we know?"

"We don't know them," Bethany said and then wrinkled her nose. "I don't think I want to, either."

Malia didn't say a word, which seemed odd to Bethany. Instead, Malia turned and looked back out the window. But not before Bethany had caught the troubled look on her friend's face.

two

The conversation was soon forgotten as Bethany's mother steered the minivan around the narrow cliff-side roads, passing new million-dollar homes of movie stars and the ramshackle houses of a few old-time residents. Bethany and Malia hung their heads out the windows, drinking in the rich smell of blossoming plumeria trees and laughing at wild chickens that darted quickly out of their path, hustling young chicks in front of them.

Then the road dropped down a steep incline that opened up onto a majestic bay. Bethany felt her excitement rise. At the near end of the crescent, there were only a couple of cars with empty surf racks that bore greasy stains from melted surfboard wax on their rust-eaten roofs and trunks.

Plenty of room left for us, Bethany thought happily.

Just past the cars, a long rugged point of black volcanic rock loomed out into the sea. Around that point in the ocean steamed head-high waves that marched toward the beach before suddenly pitching forward, like a huge arm reaching for shore.

Bethany spotted a surfer racing across the standing wave. She motioned for Malia to watch while he tucked himself into a ball as the lip of the wave tossed over him, placing him in the tube for a few seconds before spitting him out in a burst of spray.

"Wooo! Looks like fun, Malia! And it isn't too big—just fun size."

"I wish I hadn't hurt my shoulder playing tennis the other day!" Bethany's mother said wistfully.

"What's that you always say?" Bethany patted her mom's arm. "The apple doesn't fall too far from the tree!"

Bethany winked, and Malia laughed. The wind and waves had erased whatever it was that was troubling her, and Bethany could tell her best friend was itching to hit the surf.

Within moments, the van was parked, sunscreen applied, surfboards waxed up, and the girls were trotting quickly along the sand toward the paddle-out spot.

Bethany glanced over her shoulder as her mom pulled out the video camera and tripod from the back of the van. She gave her mother one last wave, and her mom waved back before turning to talk with a group of tourists who were slowly encircling her. Bethany shook her head as she continued to jog toward the ocean.

Bethany still didn't get it—all the attention of people wanting to have their pictures taken with her and wanting her autograph. She didn't get it, but she was trying.

"What an awesome opportunity you've been given!" she remembered her mom whispering to her after an interview at the hospital. "To share your faith with so many—people you might have never met if this hadn't happened."

Yet, she didn't know how she was going to help someone else when she was just learning how to help herself.

Bethany felt Malia reach for her hand as their bare feet slapped on wet sand—time to pray. Malia had picked up the habit from Bethany—and Bethany from her father, when she was first learning to surf.

The prayer was simple. Bethany, aloud and without shame, thanked God for his creation and for the privilege of enjoyment he had given. Then she asked that he would give them his protection while in the water.

Considering what she had gone through only a year ago, the request had a powerful ring to it—one that seemed to hang in the air between them for a moment.

"Amen," both girls said at the same time and then laughed and sprinted out into the waves.

The first twenty feet of ocean bottom was covered with thick, large-grained sand. After that, it was replaced by coral-encrusted rocks that fanned out into a sharp reef. The girls quickly scrambled onto their boards as the bottom turned rocky, and then they paddled toward their surfer's playground on a riptide.

Rips, as they're known by surfers, are spent waves that create their own pathway back to the ocean in a kind of a reverse but under-the-surface river. They also cause the greatest danger for visitors, small children, or those unfamiliar with the ways of the ocean. Most people who have drowned in the waters around Hawaii stepped into a riptide and were dragged out to sea by an invisible surge far too strong to swim against.

Surfers like Bethany and Malia, with their greater understanding of the ocean and its dangers, often use a rip to get a free ride out to the action.

The girls ended their trip on the rip by racing each other to the lineup, laughing and duck diving under several clean but not terribly powerful waves along the way.

The other faces in the water were familiar ones—like Pete, the old-school guy on a thick, long board who actually surfed wearing a baseball cap to protect his balding head. To keep track of his hat, Pete had leashed it to his leather necklace. The other surfer watching the next set of waves was Eddie, a hefty, dark Hawaiian guy who spoke thick pidgin English with a happy smile.

"Hey, Bethany!" Eddie said as the girls paddled by him.

"Hey," Bethany chirped back in greeting.

Bethany paddled out farther than the others. She was gunning for the larger of the waves, and from her experience at this surf spot, she knew exactly what objects on the beach to line up with in order to get the most exhilarating ride.

She didn't have to wait long. A bump in the water appeared on the horizon and raced toward the surfers. Bethany guessed that the second or third wave would be larger than the first. She scrambled toward the bump that was now taking the shape of a swell by pulling powerfully with her right arm and compensating for the pull toward the right by correcting with the lean of her body.

The first wave rolled under her board, unbroken. The second wave stacked up in front of her. This was the one!

Bethany spun her board toward shore and paddled hard. Like a plane racing down the runway, she paddled hard into the wave. When it hit the shallow reef, the wave suddenly jacked straight up. The offshore winds tore away at the lip of the wave, casting off a plume of spray. Bethany took one last stroke and felt the bottom fall away. This was the critical point—the takeoff.

With years of experience that made the difficult look effortless, Bethany planted her hand flat on her board and did a one-hand push-up. Then in one lightning-quick movement she drew her legs beneath her and bounced to her feet as both she and the surfboard dropped down the face of the wave.

Now planted firmly on her feet with a strong but elegant stance, Bethany let gravity take her past the vertical face of the wave and out into the flat water before throwing her weight and speed into a hard bottom turn that threw a sheet of spray into the air.

Rising back to face the wave, Bethany found what surfers call the *sweet spot*—the place where the wave has the most speed and where the prospects of the wave curling over her in a tube were the most likely.

Bethany's heart soared! She was born for this. The wave stood up all the way across the end of the cove as it unwrapped on the shallow reef. A stall or misstep now would not only create a wipeout but would toss Bethany up on the shallow, razor-sharp reef. She was unafraid.

The crest of the wave began to pitch out. Bethany tucked her body down to keep the lip from hitting her in the head, and a spinning circle of powder blue and green water enveloped her in a tube. The sound changed to a kind of hollow, gentle roar, as if she were inside of a can.

Bethany could see out the end of the barreling wave. She could see Malia smiling and hooting as she stroked out of the way and over the wave.

It lasted only a second or two, and then with a terrific burst of speed, Bethany shot out of the tube and raced down the wall of the wave, pulling huge turns off the lip of the wave and ending her ride with a magnificent attempt to break her air-borne record.

Grinning from ear to ear, Bethany rejoined her friend in the lineup. "Okay, Malia, just one more for me. I'm starving!"

"Right behind you," Malia called after her.

A medium-sized wave rolled in, and Bethany scratched toward it at an angle. Having spent a lifetime in the ocean and knowing this particular surf spot, she quickly read the incoming wave and positioned herself in the right place to catch it. A few strokes later, she was sailing past Malia, shout-ing "food!" at the top of her lungs.

Moments later, an even larger wave scooped up Malia, and after a wild ride, she swept forward in a spray of white water to join Bethany as they paddled the rest of the way to shore together.

Jenna wasn't in the mood to admit she was wrong. But she couldn't help thinking that the sun did feel pretty good and that the ocean was incredibly beautiful. She felt the ocean inviting her to wash off in its cleansing waves.

Wading in up to her knees, Jenna felt the strong fingers of the waves grab at her calves and try to pull her back to sea with them. She even caught a glimpse of a sea turtle as it poked its head out of the water before stroking away.

This was a first for Jenna. She had never actually been in the ocean before. Its endless expanse made even the biggest lakes she had seen at home look puny. Like the intense sun, a few rays of hope warmed her heart.

Maybe I could learn to like this place, she thought, daydreaming.

She didn't notice the two girls coming in from the surf until they were almost right on top of her. For a moment, Jenna was dumbfounded by the shock of seeing a girl her own age, dressed in a cute bathing suit, tanned and rising up out of the water…with only one arm.

Then she remembered seeing the TV reports about a girl from Hawaii who was on her way to success as a pro surfer until she lost her arm to a shark. She'd also heard about the girl's miracle comeback. *Gotta be the same girl*, Jenna thought.

"Hi," the blonde girl said. Jenna smiled shyly.

"Hi." Jenna felt her face turn as red as her hair as the girl and her friend's eyes traveled to the red mosquito bites that covered her body.

"Looks like some skeeters got to you," the blonde girl observed.

"Yeah, they attacked while I was asleep," she said. "Terrorists."

Both girls grinned at her. "Did you have a fan going?" the blonde asked.

"Fan? No...why?"

"If you set a fan up to blow on you, you won't get bit," the dark-haired girl explained.

"That's news to me," Jenna said. "Good news."

"Yeah," the blonde nodded. "It's a trick most locals know about—hotels should tell you guys that stuff."

"Oh, I'm not visiting. I live here. Well, I just moved here."

"I'm Malia," the dark-haired girl said, offering a wet hand to Jenna.

"I'm Bethany," the blonde girl said, then grinned. "I'd offer you a handshake, too, but I'm holding my board, so there's none to spare."

Jenna dusted the sand off her hand and shook Malia's hand. "I'm Jenna. Thanks for the tip about the fan. I would've needed a blood transfusion if I had to go through this for another night."

Both Bethany and Malia laughed.

"Well, see ya later," Bethany said.

"Yeah, see ya," Jenna said.

And with that, the two surfers jogged up the beach toward a woman who appeared to be waiting for them.

Jenna watched from the shoreline as the girls buried their faces in towels and pawed through an ice chest.

She noticed the tourists lounging on their cheap grass mats turning their heads toward the girls, pointing and talking among themselves.

Then she saw one of them, an older woman in a bright floral print bathing suit and floppy beach hat, pull a camera from her beach bag and wander over to the girls who were busy stuffing slabs of fruit in their mouths.

Jenna couldn't hear the conversation, but she could tell that a request for a photo was in the works.

Not long after the photo opportunity, more cars pulled up to the beach. Most had surfboards stacked on top or poking out of the rear windows or truck beds. A group of teenage girls piled out of two of the cars, laughing and greeting each other. The Hanalei Girls Surf Team—an unofficial mix of young girls of the same general age, who lived in the same area, attended the same schools, and most important, surfed together—collected their towels, small ice chests, and surfboards, and waved at the adults who had given them a ride.

The resourceful girls had phoned around and discovered that Bethany and Malia were at Kalihi-wai getting some waves and that it wasn't crowded for a change. This was Bethany's gang, the group of girls who had been her friends since childhood. These were the people who knew her and liked her before and after the loss of her arm. These were the girls who stood with her, who understood her, who accepted her for who she was and would be her friend if she went on to be a world champion surfer or if she decided to go the soul surfer route and surf only for personal enjoyment.

Becoming a part of the Hanalei Girls Surf Team wasn't easy. The girls' long history with each other had glued them into a unified force that outsiders could seldom penetrate. The Hawaiian term for them was *hui*, meaning a group, club, or gang. Because they tended to show up en masse not only to surf spots but to the movies or other events, people would often say, "Here comes that *hui* of girls!"

The girls filtered down to the sand and tossed their gear near the Hamiltons and Malia.

"Going back out?" one of them asked Bethany and Malia.

"Yeah, as soon as I finish stuffing my face," Bethany replied with full cheeks, making Malia laugh.

The rest of the girls joined in, and Jenna felt herself really smiling for the first time in a long time. She didn't mean to eavesdrop. Without realizing it, she had slowly made her way nearer to their little gathering.

She didn't know anything about the Hanalei Girls Surf Team, but she couldn't help feeling like she wanted to be a part of their world as she watched them wax up their boards and head for the ocean.

Maybe I've made too big of a deal out of this move, Jenna thought. *Maybe Mom really does know what she's doing.*

Jenna smiled wryly. Wouldn't her mother *love* to hear that!

Just then a car horn bleated from the parking lot, shaking her from her thoughts. Jenna turned to see her mother had come to pick her up.

"Did you have a good time?" her mom asked as Jenna climbed into the car.

"It was okay," Jenna admitted a bit reluctantly. "I saw a sea turtle up pretty close."

"Really?"

"Yeah, it was kinda cool. And I think I met that girl on TV who had her arm bitten off by a shark. I mean she didn't say that to me, but she surfs and obviously lives here. Her name is Bethany. That's the same girl, isn't it?"

"I think so. I'm glad you had a good time."

Jenna glanced sideways at her mom and then fell silent.

She didn't want to admit it just yet, but there *was* something wonderful and magical about the beach. She had never known that saltwater tasted so salty or that sea turtles would come in so close to the beach. She never realized how such a little wave could so easily knock you off balance or how walking on dry sand was like walking across hot coals and yet at the shoreline it could be soothing and cool.

On top of that, it was kind of cool to meet someone she'd seen on TV. And besides, that person had been *nice* to her.

What had really shocked her—and kind of excited her—was the number of *girls* who surfed.

Up until that morning at the beach, she had always thought of surfing as a guy's sport, like skateboarding or something.

Today almost every surfer was a girl—*a girl!* This was a wonderful world, full of new sensations, sights, and people.

As the car pulled into the long driveway of Jenna's new rented home, a small *ohana,* or family house constructed behind a larger home, she was hit with another thought.

"Mom, are you going to Wal-Mart anytime today?"

"Well, I have to drop off some paperwork in town. Why? Do you need something?"

"I think you ought to pick up a couple of fans," Jenna said. "I hear the local people sleep with them blowing on them because of the mosquitoes."

"I can see how it might keep you cool, but how does that help with bugs?"

"The mosquitoes don't like the breeze; it blows them away before they can land on you."

"Who knew?" Jenna's mom said with a small smile. "Sure, I'll stop and get a couple of fans."

"Oh, and you might want to get us some bug repellent too," said Jenna. "In case what I heard about the fans isn't exactly right. I'm really tired of being a Happy Meal for bugs."

Jenna's mom rolled her eyes. "Happy Meal?"

They looked at each other and then laughed— the sound surprised them both after weeks of constant bickering. They were still grinning as they took their shoes off and placed them side by side at the front door.

"By the way, what's the deal with this shoe thing?" Jenna asked.

"I think it's a Hawaiian custom. I read somewhere that you will really insult people who live here if you wear your shoes into their houses."

"Why?"

"I don't know," her mom said, "but I think it's kind of a good idea. It does keep the mud and sand out." Jenna rolled her eyes this time. "Well, when in Rome, do as the Romans do."

"Riiight," Jenna said. Then, in spite of herself, she started to wonder if her mom was right about that too.

Bethany and her friends weren't exactly Romans, but there was something different about them—something she wanted to be a part of.

She thought about them late into the night, with her new fan blowing at full strength across her bed. Even the discomfort of a few patches of sunburn, spots she had missed while greasing up, didn't bother her.

Tomorrow is Sunday, she thought sleepily. *Wish I knew what those girls will be doing... bet it's something fun.*

 *three*

Sunday morning at Bethany's house was a beehive of activity as the family prepared for church.

Bethany, her dad, and her brothers had cracked a dawn patrol at a nearby surf spot and were now quickly trying to shower, eat, and change into clean clothes before Mom herded them out the door.

"Is Malia coming to church this morning?" Bethany's mom asked in the middle of the rush.

"I dunno," Bethany said around a piece of toast. "If she can get a ride she will."

"Give her a call, and tell her we'll stop by and get her on our way," Mrs. Hamilton said, putting the juice back in the fridge. "Tell her I have a couple of books from the *Chronicles of Narnia* to give her too."

Soon, the entire family piled into the van and bumped down the road to Malia's house. Even though Noah and Tim were old enough to drive and had their own cars, it was a tradition to go to church as a family.

"Sunday is family day," their parents had long ago told the kids. Over the years, in spite of busy schedules and changing lives, they had managed to stick to that idea.

The Hamilton's family church, located on the north shore, held services in a large tent on the grounds of a private school. Bethany often joked that she went to the circus church because the large blue stripes of the huge tent made it look as if there should be elephants and clowns running around as well.

Set up inside the tent were several hundred chairs and a large stage that held a full band. The edges of the tent could be rolled up to allow the cool trade winds to blow through or dropped down in case of the wild weather that sometimes blew rain sideways.

As the van crunched over the gravel parking lot, Bethany and Malia spotted their friends making their way across the church campus. Most of the girls were a part of the Hanalei Girls Surf Team who, like Malia, had developed an interest in God in spite of the lack of interest their parents had about spiritual things.

From between two cars, a young woman popped out and waved furiously at the Hamiltons. It was Sarah Hill. Sarah served as youth director for the church and was also one of the main reasons so many young surf girls had come to know Christ.

"Bethany! Malia!" Sarah shouted.

Bethany smiled. It was fun going to youth group meetings during the week—a lot more fun than most people realized. Sarah had helped her see that faith in Christ wasn't about following a list of rules or just believing because your parents believed. It was about hanging close and personal with the most loving person in the universe—God.

Bethany and Malia quickly picked up their pace across the parking lot when they heard the worship band warming up. Church time!

People of every shape and size and from every walk of life trickled out of cars and trucks to join them in their trek to the big top. Men were dressed in aloha shirts, shorts, and rubber slippers or sandals. Some women showed up with skirts or dresses, but compared to mainland attire, they were all very casual—a dress code that was a big part of the island style. Anyone with a tie would stand out like a sore thumb. Anyone with a suit and tie would look as if he came from another planet.

Wet surfboards strapped high on top of car roofs were proof of pre-church surf sessions, and freshly waxed boards waited expectantly to grab some waves after the service.

Sarah Hill slid up next to Bethany and Malia as they walked toward the tent opening.

"Are you coming to the Get Outta School barbecue this evening?" she asked.

"Get Outta School? I almost forgot!" Bethany said.

"That's because you never go to school," said Malia.

"I do too! I go to school at my kitchen table every day."

Malia rolled her eyes as if to say, *Tough life!*

"Actually, I kind of miss public school," Bethany said. "I just can't keep up if I'm traveling and training."

"You can come to the barbecue anyway," Sarah smiled. "It's for the whole youth group to say hello to summer and goodbye to school."

"You can count me in," said Malia.

"I'll be there too," Bethany said. "You don't think I'd miss a chance to taste your famous strawberry pie!" Sarah was known for her secret recipe for strawberry pie, which appeared at the end of every youth gathering.

"You'll have to get behind me," Malia said with a grin.

"Pie junky," Bethany shot back.

"Great!" Sarah laughed as the girls arrived at the tent entrance. "I'll see you tonight, if not before."

After church, the Hamiltons returned home, where Bethany and Malia quickly made tropical smoothie lunches out of mango, pineapple, banana, and guava juice. As soon as their straws sucked the bottom of their glasses, the girls hustled off to load their surfboards in the car and change into swim gear.

"Timmy, will you drive us to Pine Trees?" Bethany asked. Her brother grinned at her.

"Sure, if you make me a smoothie."

"Come on," Bethany pleaded. "We wanna get in the water as soon as we can, so we can make it back in time for the barbecue tonight."

"Guess you better start walking then," Tim said with a smile.

Bethany weighed the trade-off for only a moment before she decided that it was fair enough. Then she hurried over to the blender and started assembling the ingredients for another smoothie.

"You can make one for me too!" came a voice from the back of the porch. It was Noah, the oldest of the Hamilton kids.

"No problem," sang Bethany, "but you have to clean everything up!"

There was silence as Noah weighed the trade-off in *his* mind.

"All right," Noah sighed. "I guess that's fair."

Bethany pushed the button on the blender, and it roared to life, slicing and then mashing the fruit and juice into a thick, delicious fluid.

A few moments later, smoothie in hand, Tim backed his car out of the driveway while Bethany hung her head out of the window to smell the perfume of the plumeria trees that lined the entrance to her home.

What a cool day, Bethany thought happily. Then, with no warning, she suddenly heard the voice of that young girl who had yelled at her mother run through her head: *"You don't care!"*

"Tim, did you ever yell at Mom or Dad?" Bethany asked, suddenly. She saw Malia glance up.

"Why would you ask me something like that?" said Tim.

"I overheard a girl and her mom arguing the other day, and they said terrible things to each other." Bethany frowned. "Now I can't stop thinking about it."

"Yeah, well, some people yell like that," Tim said as he studied the road ahead.

"Maybe, but they probably yell at home where nobody can hear them instead of in the grocery store parking lot," Bethany pressed.

"I yelled at Mom once."

"Really?" Bethany said, glancing back at Malia with a look that said, *Tim*? She looked back at her brother. "What happened?"

"It was a long time ago, so I don't remember all the details. But I do remember that I yelled something kinda bad at her—some word I heard other kids saying at school. I don't even know if I knew what it meant, but I knew you weren't supposed to say it. In the end, I had to spend a lot of time picking weeds." Tim grimaced. "It was terrible. My friends would come over to play, and I had to send them away. I would get up, eat, and then pick weeds until it was time to go to bed."

"How long did that last?"

"Three or four years."

"Seriously!" Bethany said, and Tim smiled.

"Long enough to learn my lesson," he answered finally. Uncharacteristically, big brother Tim reached over and put his hand on her shoulder as she and Malia started to pile out of the car. "You gotta understand something, Bethany. We're Christians—not every family has that. Because some people don't have God in their lives, they aren't able to see things the way we do."

"I know that," Bethany said a bit impatiently.

"No, I don't think you do," Tim said as she started to shut the door.

Bethany frowned at her brother—but Malia gave him a small smile of gratitude.

A few hours later, returning sandy and salty from the beach, the girls raced for the Hamilton's outdoor shower to rinse off.

"You owe me another smoothie," Tim shouted after them.

"Sorry! Only one per customer!" Bethany called out as she plunged under the spray of the showerhead.

Within a few minutes, wet bathing suits were drying on the line and the girls, hair still clingy wet, were dressed and ready for the youth group barbecue.

"I'll take you," Mrs. Hamilton offered.

"Thanks, Mom!"

"And I won't even make you fix me a smoothie," her mom added. "At least not today."

"Shoot, Bethany," Malia said. "I need to learn how to make smoothies as good as you. You have this taxi service sewn up tight!"

"That's because mine are the best," Bethany said with a delighted laugh.

"It's true!" added her mother.

"Secret sauce," Bethany advised. "Mom, did you know that Malia will soon be a professional smoothie maker?"

"What do you mean?"

"I got a summer job at Hanalei Harry's Smoothie Shack," said Malia.

"Good for you," Mrs. Hamilton said with a wink. "Watch out, Bethany, you have competition now!"

Soon the van pulled into the crowded driveway of Sarah's house. Cars were parked on both sides of the narrow street and even on the lawn in front of the youth director's house. It was a necessity in rural Hawaii, but thankfully, the tropical conditions made lawns as tough as nails and virtually bulletproof.

The delicious smell of cooking meat wafted through the air, and the chatter and laughter from dozens of conversations competed with the sound of contemporary Christian music rolling out of the stereo.

As soon as the girls hopped out of the van, Bethany's stomach growled. A smoothie lunch was no match for a couple hours of hard surfing, and the aroma was almost too much to take.

Young people stood in small knots both inside and outside Sarah's house. The conversations were all pretty similar—summer plans and school reminiscences. Some kids, reflecting on the past year like book reviewers, were trading stories about the personalities of various teachers and which classes were toughest.

Just outside the back steps of the house stood a small cluster of girls. They were dressed in the kind of clothes made popular in surf magazines. Tanned, with sun-kissed hair, they chatted with casual elegance. They laughed and talked as if they were longtime friends. Many were part of the Hanalei Girls Surf Team.

Bethany and Malia joined the conversation as everyone made plans for the summer: trips to the mainland, surf explorations on the other side of the island, and countless overnight stays at each other's homes.

"Did you hear that Brooke moved up here from the south side?" Monica announced.

"Really?" Bethany said.

"Her dad transferred jobs to this side of the island, and with the price of gas, they thought it would be better just to move over," replied Monica.

"That's cool," said Bethany. "She's a pretty good surfer."

"Yeah, well, I hope she doesn't think that just because she's living on this side of the island, she can be part of us!" said Monica defiantly.

Bethany said nothing. She had mixed feelings about the "us and them" attitude a number of the girls carried. Part of her appreciated the tightly knit *hui* and the long and deep friendships that came with it. She was glad for the loyalty of these friends and didn't want to lose it by inviting others to join the group.

At the same time, she remembered Sarah Hill's teachings about the danger a group faces when it becomes too exclusive or turns into a snobby clique.

The conversation trailed away as everyone loaded paper plates with burgers, chili, rice, and salad.

After the meal, Sarah squeezed all her students into the living room. Sitting on a stool in the corner, she opened her Bible and read to them these words from Matthew 13:44: "The kingdom of heaven is like treasure hidden in a field. When a man found it, he hid it again, and then in his joy went and sold all he had and bought that field."

Bethany was surprised to see Sarah look up from her Bible at *her*. After a long, thoughtful moment, Sarah glanced around at the rest of the group.

"Wherever you go this summer and whatever you end up doing," Sarah continued, "God may put people in your life who need to discover the terrific treasure a relationship with God can be. He may also put treasure in your path that you don't recognize. In fact, sometimes the treasure is kinda crusty and ugly-looking on the surface, but after you wash off the dirt, you find the real value there. God may want to use you as a guide to bring someone else to his treasure field or even as a prospector to discover treasure around you."

Bethany nodded and then glanced at her friends. She enjoyed Bible studies, even though she often found it difficult to concentrate for long periods of time.

I think I have the attention span of a lightning bolt, Bethany thought with a pang of guilt.

Sarah was one of the few people who held Bethany's attention when she taught from the Bible. *Thankfully, it was a very short talk tonight,* Bethany thought. Sarah soon closed in prayer, and the race was on for strawberry pie.

Malia was a dessert nut. About the only dessert Bethany really enjoyed was Sarah's homemade strawberry pie, probably because it was thick with fruit. So it was a bit of a disappointment when she finally made her way to the dessert table to find the pie tin empty.

Other kids were greedily gobbling up the other kinds of dessert, but none of them held any interest for Bethany. She gave a little sigh and went to return her unused plate and utensils.

It was then that she saw Malia trying to hide herself in the corner. On her dessert plate were not one, but two large pieces of Sarah's famous strawberry pie.

Bethany strolled over to her friend. "Guess what? The pie was all gone before I even got to it!"

Malia said nothing. One piece of her pie was almost finished, the other untouched. The two girls locked eyes for a moment. It was really not a big thing—it was only a piece of pie. Malia was normally a gracious and generous girl, but as anyone could see, strawberry pie was her weakness. Bethany knew she didn't *need* a piece of pie. In fact, none of the kids *needed* a piece of pie. But here was her good friend having a moment of greedy, self-centered delight.

"Grrrrrrr." The sound came out of Bethany softly at first. "Grrrrrrr-raaaR!" she roared. The sound of a lion, a very unhappy lion.

Malia slowly smiled at Bethany. "Okay, okay. You're right!" she said in a way that seemed almost like a confession. She slipped the piece of pie onto Bethany's clean plate with a sigh. "I knew I was being a pig. Thank you for growling at me, though."

"That's what friends are for," Bethany said. "True friends!"

They grinned at each other and then joined in with the swirl of students who were still talking excitedly about the summer ahead of them.

Just two miles away, Jenna dug through her old suitcase of clothes, trying her best not to cry. The morning had started off pretty well—at least there weren't any new mosquito bites to deal with. But as the day wore on, she felt more and more depressed ... and alone. Her mom had evidently decided it was more important to spend Sunday with her new boyfriend.

What was I thinking? That some miracle would happen and those girls would just come find me and invite me to go with them somewhere?

Jenna shoved the clothes into the dresser drawers, not really caring where or how they landed. She stopped only long enough to swipe angrily at the tears streaming down her face.

Who cares, anyway!? She felt the shout rise up in her.

Then something strange happened. She remembered something her dad said to her years ago ... before he died. She could hear his voice now like a thought inside her head.

Even though I won't always be here to take care of you, remember, *God has plans for you—a future for you ... full of hope.*

 *four*

The first morning of summer vacation drowned out any hope for a day in the sun. The massive storm system that came rolling in from the south drenched the island with heavy sheets of rain and caused a collective sigh to echo across the island from kids who had anxiously awaited their first day of freedom.

Bethany heard the raindrops pelt hard against her bedroom window. This was the kind of day for staying in bed, not for going to the beach. In spite of that thought, she threw her covers back and slipped out of bed.

Pro surfers had to train in both good weather and bad. It was a good idea, really. A lot of contests were held in less than ideal weather conditions. And with a local contest scheduled for this weekend, she had to keep in top form.

But it *was* raining miserably.

She almost fell back in bed and pulled the sheets back over her head. It was tempting, but she willed herself to get up.

Her mother's knock at her door came a few short minutes later, and within half an hour, Bethany and her mom were splashing through puddles on their drive to the beach.

Pulling up to the surf spot called Pine Trees, Bethany saw that the stiff offshore wind was creating extremely choppy conditions. Gusts snapped off the top of forming waves, billowing spray high into the air after each peak.

Bethany frowned.

"Ugh!" her mother said, echoing her thoughts. "Think I'll stay in the van with a good book. Don't forget, I have to be at my dentist appointment in an hour, kiddo."

Bethany nodded and slipped out of the car. As she lifted up the rear van door, she wondered why on earth she hadn't just stayed in bed. She probably could've just skipped today. But some inner strength pushed her to keep going in spite of herself.

"Never know where God will lead you—or what you might learn, Bethany," her dad liked to say. She smiled as she dug around for her wet suit top.

"This'll help," she said under her breath, feeling a little better about the day as she quickly slipped the top over her head.

Bethany slid her surfboard from the rack, bent her head away from the driving rain, and trotted toward the surf. *In a few seconds I'll be wet anyway, so this rain doesn't matter.*

There was only one other surfer in the water as she plunged into the warm, stormy sea. *He's violating the rule about surfing alone*, Bethany thought. She hoped more surfers showed up despite the rain.

Bethany's first wave was surprisingly fun, considering the conditions. The hard offshore winds were acting as an unseen hand, pushing back against the tumbling wave just long enough so that Bethany could squeeze into the tube and shoot out again. With every turn she hurled huge arcs of spray into the air, which were carried away by the trade winds.

Finally, another car pulled into the parking lot, windshield wipers banging away furiously. She felt several pairs of eyes on her as she performed the graceful water ballet.

Bethany was relieved to see two middle-age men paddle into the lineup on long boards—even if it meant sharing the best waves. *Thank you, God!* It was uncomfortable surfing with just one other person, especially when she didn't know the skill of the other guy catching the waves.

In a mad dash to escape the heavy sheets of rain, Malia ducked under the awning of the smoothie stand to report for the first day of her summer job.

"At least this weather will give you time to learn your job without customers getting all impatient with you, like they did me," her boss said with a grin. Malia wiped the rain off her face with a paper towel.

Malia's boss explained that her job would be to slice up fresh fruit, clean the blenders, and make smoothies for customers. But because the smoothie stand offered little shelter from the rain, it was virtually empty most of the morning—except for a few locals who drove up in their cars and ordered smoothies for the road.

By lunchtime, her boss felt confident enough to let Malia run the stand alone. No sooner had her boss left than Bethany showed up.

Malia had her back turned, so Bethany shouted out, "I'd like 145 banana mango smoothies, *delivered*!"

Malia spun around with a grin. "I knew it was you!"

Bethany, who had been surfing all morning in spite of the rain, shivered as she sat on one of four stools tucked under the eaves of the stand. She'd asked her mom to drop her off with her bike just in case it cleared up. Bethany was starting to wonder just how smart that was.

"How's the first day on the job?" she asked.

"Kinda easy. My boss already left me alone to run the shop. Want a smoothie? I'm almost as good as you now!"

"No, actually I want something hot," Bethany said, trying to control her shivering. "But once I warm up, I'll take a chance."

"No chances—it's a sure thing!" said Malia.

"What? Are you working on commission?"

"No, but I want to see if the smoothie master approves of my work."

"All I've got is wet money; will you take it?" Bethany asked, holding out a limp five dollar bill to Malia.

"Do I have a choice?"

"No!" Bethany laughed, snatching the five out of Malia's reach. "I'm going across the street to get some *siamen* to go, first. We'll do the deal when I get back."

Grinning, Bethany ran through the rain to the restaurant on the other side of the street. Safely inside, she leaned against the door and watched the rivulets of water pour off of the roof and into the street.

What a lousy first day of summer!

Suddenly, an older model sedan—tan with a cracked taillight—came to an abrupt stop in the street. Even though the windows were rolled up and fogged, a sign that the air-conditioning was not working, Bethany could hear a familiar voice. The voice was shouting...again.

Only this time the girl got out of the car, and with a few tense words to her mother, she slammed the door, pulled the hood of a light sweatshirt over her head, and stomped off.

Bethany rolled her eyes. *No excuse for acting like that,* she thought, feeling a little righteous indignation. She had forgotten Sarah's words from the night of the barbecue.

The screen door of the kitchen slapped shut, and a slender Hawaiian guy handed Bethany a large foam bowl, steaming with noodles, and a pair of chopsticks.

"Thank you," Bethany said as she traded soggy money for the soup. She was just about to head out the door with her food when Monica walked in.

"Hey, Monica," Bethany smiled. "I was just about to head over to Hanalei Harry's so Malia could whip me up a smoothie."

"Hey back. I was going to order something to go. Why don't we just eat it here and head across the street for a smoothie with Malia after?"

"Sounds like a plan."

After wandering around Hanalei town for a while, Jenna started looking for a place to grab something to drink. It was then that she noticed Hanalei Harry's Smoothie Shack. She quickly eyed the menu and glanced up to find Malia grinning back at her.

"Didn't I meet you the other day at the beach? You were with that Bethany girl," Jenna said shyly, feeling her spirits rise a little. The fight with her mom had been bad—so bad that she'd wondered briefly about trying to find a way back to Arizona.

"Yeah!" Malia nodded. "You were the one with the mosquito war story. Did you get a chance to pick up some fans?"

"Yep," Jenna said, taking a seat on one of the stools. She held up her arms to display only a few faded welts. "Works like a charm."

"Sweet," said Malia.

"I've gotta live here—but I don't have to be on the menu, right?"

Malia laughed. "Where're you from?"

"Arizona," Jenna said, warming to the girl's laughter. "But not the desert part. I came from the mountains. I always have to explain that 'cause most people don't realize there are mountains in Arizona."

"I always think of it as a desert," Malia admitted. "So you like it there better, and your mom made you move or something?"

"My mom…" Jenna's words trailed off. "It's nice here, nicer than I thought, but I had to leave all my friends, my horse, my house, everything."

Malia sensed there was a story this customer wanted to share.

"Let me get this smoothie for you, and you can hang out and tell me all about you," Malia offered kindly.

"Thanks," Jenna said, suddenly feeling like she wanted to open up and share. There was something different about Malia—something good that made it okay to talk.

For the next half hour Jenna told Malia her tale of frustration about leaving everything comfortable and familiar for the unwelcome trip to Hawaii—all so her mom could continue a relationship with a man she had met.

Her anger at the whole situation simmered just below the surface, but during her conversation, she managed not to say terrible things about her mom to Malia.

"I really miss my horse...and my friends," Jenna said.

"You'll make new friends," Malia assured her. "It's tougher during the summer to connect, but hang around the beach, and it won't be long. Hey, you met us the first day, didn't you?"

"Yeah, I guess so," Jenna said, feeling better.

While Jenna talked, the rain-filled clouds drifted away and the sun peeked out of blue holes in the sky. Soon there was enough sun to dry up puddles and make the idea of lounging on the beach attractive again.

"Well, I've taken enough of your time," said Jenna. "I think I'll go hang out on the beach."

"Sounds like a plan," said Malia. "See you around." She picked up the empty smoothie glass. "Hey, Jenna! You ought to come to the surf contest this Saturday at Pine Trees. It's really fun."

Jenna had no idea where Pine Trees Beach was located, so Malia pointed out directions from the Smoothie Shack.

"Maybe Bethany and I can give you some surfing lessons," Malia offered.

"That would be great!" Jenna said.

Later, as Jenna walked down to the beach, it seemed that the whole day had taken on a new glow. Malia would have been surprised to know just how much her few words of kindness had meant to this new girl.

For Jenna, the fact that there was one person on this whole mosquito-infested island who was willing to talk to her, to ask questions about her life, her likes, her experiences, was exhilarating.

After having such a bad fight with her mother and suddenly hearing her dad's voice, she'd wondered if she was going crazy. But now she knew she wasn't.

She felt like she might just have a future—and a hope.

Jenna had only been gone a few moments when Bethany and Monica showed up at the smoothie shack.

"This place is cool," Monica said, looking around.

"Hey guys! Ready to be blown away by my ultimate smoothies?" Malia asked as soon as they plunked down on their stools.

"I brought you another victim, didn't I?" Bethany shot back. Malia grinned wickedly.

"Hey, you'll never guess what I saw earlier," Bethany went on. "The same car from the shopping center. You know...the one where that girl was going off on her mom. And guess what? The girl is still going off today."

"She was here," Malia said.

"Who?"

"That girl you heard yelling at her mom."

"No way! She didn't go off on you, did she, for not putting the straw deep enough in the smoothie or something?" Bethany winked at Monica, but Malia frowned.

"She actually seems kinda nice. What's really funny is she's the same girl we met on the beach the other day—the one with the mosquito bites."

"Hmm. Maybe she was nice to you," Bethany said. "But in my book really nice people don't scream and yell at other people, especially their parents."

"Well, that's easy for you to say. Don't you remember what Tim said? Maybe she just hasn't been taught by parents like yours." Malia looked Bethany in the eye. "My parents aren't saints, either, remember?"

"But you didn't hear the stuff that girl was saying!" Bethany argued, avoiding her friend's stare. "I just can't imagine how anyone could treat her mother that way. I mean, I know it happens. I just don't like it, and I'm not really all fired up about hanging out with someone like that. Now how about that smoothie?"

Malia shrugged and pointed to the menu board. "Take your pick," she said. "Anyhow, I invited her to come to the surf contest on Saturday."

"O—kay," said Bethany slowly, sensing there was more to the story.

"And...well...see, I said that maybe we could give her some lessons," Malia admitted almost apologetically.

"We?" Bethany said incredulously. "You got a mouse in your pocket?"

Monica laughed.

"Come on!" Malia said. "You're always giving surf lessons to someone...even to the kookiest people."

"We're surfing in that contest, Malia!"

"Yeah, I know, but there's always a lot of free time after our heats."

"Why did you commit me?" Bethany asked finally.

"Because she met you, she heard about you, you were friendly to her," Malia reminded her with a pleading look.

"That was before I saw what she was really like," Bethany replied. "Besides, you don't need my help, you can teach her yourself. After all, she's *your* friend."

Malia sensed something odd in the way Bethany said that last line, but she decided to shrug it off. Bethany was not the type to get jealous if other friends came into the picture, but she *was* very careful about what kind of friends she chose to hang out with herself.

Monica, who had been listening to the exchange between Malia and Bethany, decided to add her two cents' worth.

"Malia, I know that you and Bethany are always picking up strays and dragging them around with you, but you've gotta remember that we've got to keep the Hanalei Girls Surf Team *special!*"

"I'm not saying to make her part of the team or anything," Malia protested. "I'm just trying to be helpful to a new kid on the island."

"Yeah, well, if you start giving some kid surf lessons, the next thing you know she'll want to hang out with us all the time, and we don't even know her."

"And I'm not sure I want to know her," tossed in Bethany. "The stray Malia found seems to have fleas."

"Just be careful who you invite to hang out with us," Monica added.

"Yeah, okay, we'll just play it by ear," said Malia, stung by the less than charitable reaction from her friends. "So, what kind of smoothie magic do you want me to mix up for you?"

"I dunno. They all look so good!" said Monica. "How am I supposed to decide?"

Jenna's mom showed up late to pick her up at the beach. Instead of getting mad about it — or bringing up the boyfriend deal—Jenna brushed it off, feeling the new bounce in her step as she made her way over to the car.

"Good day in spite of the rain?"

"Way better than I expected!" Jenna said with a wide smile—a smile that she hoped would call a truce between them. She took a deep breath and plunged ahead. "Mom, can I go to a surf contest this Saturday?".

"Well, if you get your chores done and if you promise not to go out too far—"

"Mom! I'm not five years old anymore!" Jenna said, exasperated. She paused and then tiptoed on thin ice. "And I'd *really* like a new bathing suit."

"What's wrong with your old one?!"

"Nothing, really. I ..." Jenna frowned. "They just wear different stuff than we did back in Arizona." Her mom pursed her lips, staring straight ahead as she drove.

"Money doesn't grow on trees, you know."

"Please, Mom? Please? I'll even work for it if you want."

"Well," her mom said, glancing over as a small smile formed on her lips, "let's see how much they are when we get to town."

"Okay," Jenna said eagerly, "but I think you have to buy them at a surf shop, and there's a surf shop just up the road."

As the car pulled onto the highway, Jenna caught a glimpse of herself in the side mirror. It was an image she hadn't seen in awhile. It was a girl smiling.

five

Bethany couldn't help smiling. After a couple days of rain, the sun had crawled out from behind the clouds, the trade winds wound down, and the island returned to the warm, sunny paradise made famous on so many postcards. It was awesome surfing weather.

Floating on the water, she felt her excitement build as she spotted the large swell coming toward her. While most girls tended to back away from bigger surf, she came alive in it. Bethany waited for the perfect moment and then pitched herself over the face of the wave, using gravity to sweep her down the wave as she simultaneously sprang to her feet.

Moments later, she shot forward toward shore in an impressive spray of white water that seemed to glint like diamonds in the bright sun. *What an awesome day!* she thought happily.

Bethany was so relieved that she didn't have to work out in the rain again. She was even more relieved when she saw Monica waving at her from her beach cruiser in the parking lot. Bethany had been training like crazy for the contest and was looking forward to taking a little break.

She also needed someone to talk to. Malia had been working so much they hadn't had a chance to get together, so Bethany had been left to deal with her thoughts by herself. Not fun.

After quickly packing her surf gear in the back of her mom's van, Bethany and Monica were off, pedaling their beach cruisers down the coconut palm-tree-lined road that led to Hanalei Bay Pier. Glimpses of turquoise water flashed past them between the rows of expensive homes.

"Wouldn't it be great to live in one of these houses?" Monica said dreamily.

"Yeah, until a tsunami came," Bethany answered wryly. "Remember the story of the house built on sand?"

"Sure, I remember that story, but the guy had a great view while it lasted," Monica laughed.

The bikes wheeled down a bumpy little path and then onto the concrete deck of the pier. Along the edge of the pier, old men and women with brown wrinkled faces hidden under large floppy hats fished with cane poles. At the end of the pier was a large roofed pavilion with a stainless steel ladder reaching down into the water. In a former life, the pier had been a hub of shipping activity, but now it served primarily as a tourist attraction and viewpoint for those wanting to watch beginners catch the small waves that brushed under its pilings.

Most island children saw the pier as a launch pad and would jump together in groups, laughing wildly as they cannonballed into the warm ocean only to scramble back up the ladder and do it again.

Bethany and Monica laid their bikes down at the end of the pier and stared into the water.

"Look!" Bethany pointed. "Hammerheads!"

Sure enough, baby hammerhead sharks, about a foot in length, darted in and out of the pilings.

"That's nuts!" said Monica.

"Haven't you ever seen them before? They're here a lot," Bethany said.

"They're too small to hurt you, aren't they?"

"Yeah, right now they're way more afraid of you than you should be of them. Give them a few years to grow and it will be the other way around."

"I wonder where their mommy is?"

"Sharks don't make good moms; they give birth and swim off," Bethany said thoughtfully as she stared down into the water. "The mom is probably a long way away."

"I hope so," Monica said, glancing back at Bethany.

"I hope so too."

"And all those guys," Monica said, pointing to the surfers in the water, "really hope so."

"Did you know that sharks eat other sharks?"

"No. Why would they do that?"

"Cannibals," Bethany said, wrinkling her nose in disgust. "They'll even eat their own family and friends."

"Sharks have friends?"

"Uh, no, I guess not." Bethany laughed. "But if they did, they would eat them."

The girls stared silently at the small sharks for a while, and as they did, Bethany felt troubled thoughts swirl through her mind again. She looked up at her friend.

"Monica, I think we have to be careful that we don't make our *hui* so tight that we hurt other people."

"What do you mean?" Monica said in surprise. "You aren't saying that we should just let any poser or wannabe hang out with us?"

"I don't know exactly what I'm saying," Bethany answered. She suddenly felt an uncomfortable feeling—kind of like a nudge. She sighed and went on. "I mean, I really value having close friendships with all my friends in the Hanalei Girls Surf Team, but I think we have to be really careful. Maybe we should be more open to people that God would want us to invite in."

"What if God wanted us to invite everyone into our crew?" Monica asked, narrowing her eyes a little.

"I don't know if he would ask that, but if he did, I don't think we would have much choice."

"Are you trying to include that friend of Malia's into our group? The girl doesn't even surf! I would rather invite Brooke from the south side."

"No, I'm not saying that. I just think that even though we've gotta keep our friendship tight, we gotta still be willing to be friendly and make friends with other people."

"How are we going to do that?" asked Monica.

"I dunno. I can't explain it, but it's like I keep getting this feeling the past two days that I can't get rid of—like God's trying to talk—but I haven't been listening."

Bethany frowned, suddenly feeling confused and more than a little embarrassed under Monica's sharp stare. "Or something like that..."

The bike ride home was a scenic one but a quiet one too, as the girls bounced along unpaved roads under huge canopies of bright green trees, both lost in their thoughts.

At the entrance to a golf course they parted company, and Bethany started the short pedal to her home while Monica had the longer trek to the condominiums she lived in up the road.

Bethany still felt troubled, but she decided for the time being to force their conversation to the back of her mind. She had Saturday's contest to think about, after all...and what was more important than that?

six

Early Saturday morning the promoters were already setting up the judging tents, and vendors were staking out their sections of the beach and parking lot where they would be selling food, beverages, and souvenirs to the crowd.

Soon a long procession of cars, with surfboards stacked on their roofs, made their way to the Pine Trees parking lot. The water quickly filled with contestants getting in practice runs, while the beach sprouted umbrellas and sand chairs like multicolored mushrooms. Cars pulled up and dropped off spectators and contestants alike, who were prepared for the day with ice chests, beach chairs, and surf gear.

A few miles away, the Hamilton household was on full alert.

In the garage, Bethany's dad, Tom, was selecting the right surfboards from a quiver of water vehicles. Having a backup board was essential in the event of changing surf conditions or board breakage.

Noah checked and rechecked his camera gear and unplugged oversized camcorder batteries from their charger and stuffed them into a backpack. His role, with help from Tim, would be to take pictures and video of Bethany's surfing. The images from this contest would go to sponsors and on his sister's website, and they would provide Bethany with footage to polish her style.

Tim hauled ice chests to the car that his mom had filled with every conceivable goodie. Hawaiians follow a "my ice chest, your ice chest" tradition, meaning whatever you bring to the beach is fair game for all your friends and acquaintances. Bethany's mom had packed accordingly.

Meanwhile, Bethany debated about what to wear from a number of bathing suits that had been donated to her by a sponsor. At the last minute she decided on a red, white, and blue combination and ran into the bathroom to change as her dad hollered from the van to hurry up.

Nothing like rushing me when I'm nervous, she thought as she scrambled out of the house and into the van.

Soon the Hamilton crew, surrounded by surfboards, ice chests, camera gear, and beach chairs, clattered across the small single-car bridge that marked the entrance to the Hanalei valley.

Bethany heard her dad breathe a heavy sigh of relief as they finally escaped the mass exodus of traffic by pulling into the driveway of a family friend.

"Cheri, which one is our firstborn? Because I think we should give him to the McCoys for letting us park here."

"It's a small price for a good parking space," her mom grinned.

"The least we could do," Bethany added, trying to sound innocent—until she winked at Noah and everyone laughed.

Before the family exited the car, Dad held up his hand. "Hey! Before everything gets going, let's pray." Bethany lowered her head with the rest of her family.

"Lord," their dad prayed, "we give this whole event to you. If your name will be glorified by Bethany doing well in the contest, we ask for your help for her, and if your name will be honored better by her losing, we will be happy with that as well. We ask for safety for all those taking part today. In the name of your son, Jesus, amen!"

"Amen," echoed all the voices in the van.

The family quickly loaded their arms with gear and began their slow migration to the beach. Bethany, a single surfboard under her arm, looked over at her brother Tim, who struggled under the burden of several surfboards and an ice chest.

"Hey, Tim, there are times when having only one arm really pays off!"

Tim only grunted in return.

Once the family had established a spot on the sand, Bethany walked over to the registration table, signed in, and picked up her complimentary T-shirt. She would be surfing a bit later in the day in a heat with a friend and a couple of girls from the south side of the island.

Malia, along with a number of other girls, drifted on to the beach, and soon the Hamilton location became an encampment for all the Hanalei Girls Surf Team.

"Hurry, Mom!" Jenna shouted to the closed bathroom door. "I don't want to be late!"

"I'm going as fast as I can," said the muffled voice of her mom. "You ought to be happy that I'm getting up early to drop you off at the beach before I go to work."

Jenna caught sight of her image in the hall mirror and frowned slightly.

Like most people her age, she was not entirely pleased with what she observed. She really liked her new neon blue and green swimsuit. But she wished her hair wasn't so red and her skin didn't look so...white. Her critique of her body would have continued right down to her toes, but the bathroom door opened and her mom came out and said, "Okay, let's go!"

Following the surfboard-laden cars across the Hanalei Bridge, Jenna's mom found Pine Tree Beach easily. Jenna quickly exited the car and waved goodbye to her mother.

The beach was alive with activity and color. Bright pennants, with the names of sponsoring companies emblazoned upon them, drifted high above the tents in the gentle breeze as tanned men and women, surfboards under their arms, swarmed over the beach.

Suddenly, an air horn sounded, and four men wearing colored Lycra jerseys and holding surfboards bounded toward the water. The surf meet was on.

Jenna stood wide-eyed, taking it all in.

Bethany glanced up briefly at the sound of the air horn and then bent over to finish stretching her hamstrings. She and her friends had hiked farther down the crescent bay to a location out of the contest area in order to tune up and practice for their upcoming heats.

Doing stretching exercises on the hard sand was the first step, and the girls, although young and limber, took this part of the routine seriously. Even a slight injury could mean the difference between winning and losing in a contest with aggressive and talented competitors.

A small rectangle of wax was passed around, and the girls scraped it over the top of their surfboards in order to create an uneven surface so they wouldn't slip off.

Leashes were fastened. Those who planted their right foot in the back of their stance put their leash on that foot. Those who favored their left foot or "goofy foot," as Bethany did, hooked the leash on that one.

The rolling whitewater grabbed at the knees of the girls as they waded into deeper water. Unlike many places in Hawaii, the Pine Trees area had a smooth sandy bottom completely free of reef or rocks.

When they reached waist-deep water, the girls slid onto their boards and stroked out toward the horizon. Their objective was the smooth blue water just past the breaking point. Even though their movements looked effortless, it took stamina, skill, and a lot of practice to make it look so easy.

As the whitewater from a breaking wave exploded in front of the girls, they quickly grabbed the rail of their surfboards and, with one fluid motion, pointed the nose deep under the wave while drawing one knee under them and throwing the other foot out and up as balance.

This maneuver, if done properly, would allow the girls to dive under the power and reversing force of the wave. If done improperly, the end result could mean that they would be pushed all the way back to the beach. Bethany and her friends zipped through the crashing whitewater like pros.

For the next hour the girls raced along the face of powder blue waves, executing arcing turns and finding the tube time and time again.

Jenna, not recognizing anyone, found a spot on the sand and watched in awe as the remarkably talented, bronzed men and women took to the water in competition.

Behind her, the announcer called out a commentary on what was happening in the water and on the scores of the winners. Every few minutes the air horn would sound, indicating the start or end of a heat.

Just then, Jenna noticed a cluster of girls standing at the edge of the water. Each wore a different colored jersey. One of the girls Jenna recognized, even though her back was turned. She was tall — taller than the others. She had almost white-blonde hair, and the left sleeve of her jersey was knotted. It was Bethany, the girl she had met the week before on the beach.

The starting horn blared, and Bethany raced toward the waves, her long legs giving her a sprinting advantage that she would otherwise lose because she could only paddle with one arm.

Shortly after the shark attack and her return to a competitive career, contest judges had offered her special consideration due to her handicap. Bethany turned them down cold. She would compete at the same level, with the same rules as the rest of the girls. If she had a physical disadvantage, then she would just work harder to overcome it.

Now paddling to the take-off spot with breakneck speed, Bethany and the other girls in the heat would compete for the top seat in a good-natured but aggressive battle.

Points were given for each wave ridden and were also determined by how long a surfer stayed on the wave and how complicated the maneuvers were that were done on the wave. A surfer could win a contest by catching lots and lots of waves with the best rides of those waves being counted for points. Yet it was possible to win a contest by catching just a few waves and outperforming the competitors.

Surfers could suffer penalties as well. Taking a wave that an opponent was already riding would result in a "triangle" for the offending surfer as would shoving or pushing another surfer, trying to dismount them from the wave.

A small wave popped up, and several girls scrambled to take the point position on it. Bethany, her ocean sense honed by many hours looking at the horizon, felt before she saw that there was something more substantial than this wave. Rather than chase the small swell in, she paddled farther out.

Suddenly, a large breaker loomed up. It was one of the larger set waves of the day. Bethany smiled to herself. She knew she had the wave since the other girls were hopelessly inside and scrambling just to avoid being caught by its breaking power.

She spun her board toward shore and took several strokes with her powerful right arm. Bethany felt the bottom drop out of the wave, and she gracefully came to her feet. This wave was now hers to control.

Bethany used the speed of the drop to drive out into the flat water in front of the pitching wave and then dig hard on her inside rail to snap the board back up the face of the wave, stalling mid-way up on the breaker.

Bethany saw the wall of water stand up in front of her. She knew she had to take one of two opportunities: she could power drive across the wall and use her speed to make huge snap turns, or she could sink her back foot, stall just a moment more, and slip into the spitting tube.

With the ease of a champion, Bethany slowed her drive and let a turquoise lip of water envelop her.

On the beach, people jumped to their feet. Her dad began counting under his breath: "One thousand one, one thousand two..."

Bethany had vanished completely behind the curtain of water; only the tip of her board was visible.

"One thousand three, one thousand four, one thousand five..."

Cameras whirled and clicked.

With a huge burst of spray, Bethany exploded from inside the collapsing wave. Hoots and cheers went up, and judges, not waiting for her to finish her ride, began to scribble on their pads.

Bethany continued her drive down the wave, picking up speed, which she used in a stunning backslash maneuver, snapping back to a small floater as the wave diminished on the shore.

Bethany smiled to herself. She knew that her competitors would have a tough time matching that wave in the limited time each heat was held.

She turned her board away from the beach and paddled back for more.

On the beach, Jenna found herself on her feet, cheering for Bethany. And even though she didn't really understand a lot of what she had just seen performed, she knew it took real skill to pull it off.

The air horn sounded, and Jenna watched from a short distance away as Bethany's friends and family went down to the water's edge to congratulate her as she came sliding in on her belly.

Everyone seemed so happy for her. Jenna inched closer to the group, feeling invisible — but wanting to be a part of something that felt so... good. Jenna saw a woman that she didn't recognize laugh and toss a towel on Bethany's head as she stood up.

"Great job, kiddo!" the woman said with a smile.

"Thanks, Sarah!" Bethany said, hugging the woman.

"We're so proud of you," Bethany's mom whispered.

"Ho! You gotta come see your ride!" a young man, who must have been her brother, shouted as he replayed the video over and over to the crowd standing around him.

Jenna trailed behind them as they made their way back to the judges' tent.

"And the winner of the junior division, with an incredible barrel ride of over five seconds, is Bethany Hamilton!" sounded the loudspeaker.

Before long, Bethany was standing on the winner's platform, a beautiful lei around her neck and a *haku*, or headband lei, on her head, holding a huge trophy as the emcee continued on about the "Comeback Kid."

When the microphone came to her, Bethany said a simple thank you to God and her family and then handed it back to the fast-talking commentator and the next round of winners.

Jenna held herself back as a group of girls she didn't know surrounded Bethany. She recognized Malia in the group, but it seemed too odd—too uncomfortable—to push her way in.

She wanted to tell Bethany that she was impressed with her surfing ability and that she admired the fact that she hadn't let the shark attack stop her from her dreams. She wanted to say thank you for the small kindness shown to her. She wanted to say that she didn't know many people on the island that she could call a friend and that she hoped that Bethany and Malia might be those people.

All this was going through her head as Bethany pawed through the ice chest, looking for something. Her huge trophy lay heating up on a beach towel, and her lei, Jenna noticed, was now draped around her mom's neck.

Bethany found a large bottle of water and guzzled it down quickly and in a very unladylike way.

"Bethany!" her mom said, laughing.

Bethany smiled sheepishly and plopped down in a beach chair, bottle of water in her hand. Then she looked up—looked right at Jenna—and looked down again. But not before Jenna had seen that she recognized her.

She doesn't want to be bothered with someone like me, Jenna thought, a low, sinking feeling swirling over her.

Jenna walked away as quickly as she could, not pausing to watch the other surfers for fear someone might see the tears in her eyes. She had almost reached her own towel when she heard someone say her name.

"Jenna?"

She turned around and saw that it was Malia.

"I thought I recognized the red hair. Did you see the contest?" Malia asked excitedly.

"Yeah, sweet," Jenna swallowed and managed a cheerful smile. "And Bethany won."

"With a tube ride like that she could have fallen off on every other wave and still won," Malia said, rolling her eyes good naturedly. "So, are you still up for a surf lesson?"

Jenna studied Malia's face; she really seemed sincere.

"I would, but I'm going to have to go pretty soon." She grinned sheepishly. "And then there's the fact that I don't have a surfboard!"

Then a thought came to Jenna, a thought that bubbled up through the rejection and clung to the hope that she could still be a part of it all.

"Malia, where do you buy a surfboard?"

"New or used?"

"Oh, for sure, used," Jenna said.

"Well, usually people buy those off friends or maybe from the paper or at a garage sale. What size are you looking for?"

Jenna's face had a blank look on it, so Malia looked at her size.

"If I were you, I'd start with an eight-footer. Much longer, and it would be hard to carry, and much shorter, too hard to catch waves with it if you haven't surfed much."

"Eight foot. Okay...I can remember that."

Jenna's mom, holding shoes in her hand, approached the girls.

"Jenna, I've been looking all over the beach for you! You were supposed to be at the parking lot for me to pick you up twenty minutes ago!"

"Oh, uh, I'm sorry, Mom. I lost track of time," Jenna said, mortified that her mom had yelled at her in front of Malia.

Jenna's mom scowled at her.

"Okay, see you later," Malia said cheerfully, as if she sensed trouble brewing. "We'll give the surf lessons a rain check."

"Yeah, later," said Jenna, already turning toward the parking lot with the slow, weary shuffle of someone who's not so sure "later" was going to happen.

The ride home was unpleasant, as she'd expected, but Jenna didn't pay much attention to the lecture her mother delivered. Malia had given her back a sliver of hope, and she wasn't about to let go of it. Not yet.

She had another adventure on her mind: to buy a surfboard and learn to surf.

seven

After showering, Jenna scoured the classified section of the paper for surfboards. She found a few, but they were not the right size, and some seemed very expensive.

She piled all of her money on her bedspread and counted it several times. Including quarters, dimes, and nickels, she had just about ninety dollars saved up. If she got creative, she might make it to a hundred.

Jenna dug around for change in all the usual places: under sofa cushions and in drawers. In the end, she was a few dollars richer but still short of the hundred-dollar goal.

The next morning, a Sunday, Jenna stuffed her money in the pocket of her shorts, hopped on a bike, and started cruising the neighborhoods for garage sales.

As with many things, garage sales seem to be everywhere—until you start looking for them. Then they are as scarce as hen's teeth. Jenna stumbled upon several, but the offerings were a hodgepodge of leftover stuff with not a surfboard to be found.

She had just about finished the one-mile loop and was approaching home from the back way when she spotted a hand-lettered sign stuck in a lawn that read, Garage Sale Today.

The early bargain hunters had already been at this location too. Only a few boxes of used clothing and electronic odds and ends seemed to be left. Under the shade of the eaves sat a large, dark-skinned Hawaiian man. His massive flat feet were wrapped in well-worn rubber slippers, and his thick arms were locked around a solid belly. He wore a wide smile, and his eyes danced with warmth.

Encouraged, she laid her bike on its side on the lawn and wandered into the garage. The big man turned his head, watching her.

She glanced around for a moment. No surfboards anywhere. She sighed in defeat and then turned back toward her bike.

"Can't find what you are looking for?" the big man sang out.

"No," Jenna said shyly, glancing back at him.

"Well? Maybe I can help. What you afta?"

"A surfboard."

"Ah, you gotta know for where to look, sistah," he said with a smile. "Come!"

With that he pulled his huge body off the chair and strolled into the middle of the garage. He paused, looked up at the ceiling, and pointed.

There in the rafters were surfboards of all sizes, almost a dozen of them. Jenna couldn't believe it.

"What size you looking for?"

"Eight foot," she whispered, trying not to get her hopes too high.

"I got one of dem for sure," said the big man, who produced a small rickety ladder and reached up into the rafters.

He pulled down a yellowing eight-foot board with a softly rounded nose.

"I used to ride dis years ago. Was more skinny in dem days," he added with a laugh.

"Uh, how much is this?" asked Jenna.

"Hmm. How much you have?"

"Well, I have a little over ninety-three dollars."

"As all you money?"

"Yeah, that's all my savings," Jenna said, and then rushed on. "But if you'll hold it for me, maybe I can earn some more."

"I tell you what," said the man. "You can have 'um for twenty bucks if you promise to be da best surfa in da watta."

"How can I do that?"

The man squatted a bit and looked the young redhead straight in the eyes. His voice turned merry as he said, "By having da most fun!"

On her way home, Jenna couldn't stop grinning, in spite of struggling to guide her bike with one hand, while cradling her new-used surfboard with her left.

She imagined herself gliding across the waves as she had seen Bethany do the day before. She imagined herself tanned and fit, talking with the Hanalei girls.

When Jenna got home, she put the surfboard in the backyard under a tree. The board still had a leash on it, although it was old and worn. She practiced fastening its Velcro strap on and off her ankle. She didn't know anything about being a goofy foot or a regular foot, so she tried it on both ankles to see if there was a right way to wear the thing.

Her mom was less than enthusiastic, though, when she got home and learned of Jenna's purchase.

"I don't know if just jumping into surfing is such a good idea," her mom ventured, looking over the board.

Jenna felt her new world about to drop out from underneath her.

"Why not?"

"Well, it's a dangerous sport," said her mother.

"Lots and lots of girls surf, so it can't be that dangerous."

"It's the ocean that's dangerous. And those girls know the ocean because they were raised around it. It has dangerous animals too—just ask that Bethany girl. I don't want you eaten by a shark."

"Mom!" Jenna said, feeling the tears well up in her eyes.

"Jenna, you can't...you don't..." her mother stammered, taken aback by tears instead of Jenna's usual shouting.

"I don't what?"

"Those girls are strong swimmers," her mom said finally.

"I swam every summer in the public pool back home!" Jenna said. "Besides, surfboards have a rope thing that is attached to you in case you fall off."

Jenna's mother sighed and then relented.

"I guess," she said, "if it will make you happy. But I still think we should both learn a little more about what it takes before you jump into that ocean."

"Thank you, thank you, Mom!" said Jenna gleefully. "And you don't have to worry. Those girls I told you about promised to give me lessons. So...can you take me to the beach now?

"*Now?*"

"Okay, after lunch."

"I suppose," her mother said, forcing a smile.

With that, Jenna spun away and went outside to hose the dust off her new used surfboard.

eight

Bethany spotted the Hanalei girls as soon as service was over, and she quickly made her way over to the little group that had formed around Malia. Her eyes grew wide, as she saw Malia hold a bandaged, swollen foot up for all to see.

"Shoot, Malia! What did you do to yourself?"

"I sprained my ankle last night," Malia explained with a hint of embarrassment. "Jumping on our trampoline with my sister. My timing was off. Hurt so bad when I landed on it, I thought it was broken."

"Looks like you won't be surfing with us today," Holly said.

"Nah, I can't even put a leash on this foot," said Malia. "But I may just come down and hang out."

"That's cool," Holly said. "How long do you think you'll be out of the water?"

"I dunno. As soon as I can put some real weight on it, I'll be back in."

"You want us to pick you up on the way?" Bethany offered and was surprised when Malia shook her head no.

"Nah, it's okay. If I decide to go, I'll ask my mom to drive me down."

"Okay," Bethany said, still staring at Malia. Something was wrong, but she wasn't sure what it was.

"So," Monica piped in, "if you can't surf, you have to shoot photos of us!"

"No way!" shot back Malia.

"That's the rule!" said Monica, half joking. "Those who can't surf must take photos of those who can."

"They'd all be out of focus anyway," Bethany teased, getting a small smile from Malia.

Just then, Sarah Hill walked up and said, "Malia! What in the world happened to you?"

Jenna had a dilemma.

On the advice of Malia, she had purchased an eight-foot surfboard. But now she realized that the little sedan her mother drove was not much longer than her surfboard. And the car had no racks to throw the board on.

Jenna tried everything she could think of to fit the board into the car. She laid the passenger seat flat, but the board would not squeeze into the space. She rolled the back windows down and tried to shove the board through the car sideways, but then she realized that the first passing car would no doubt snap off the nose of the surfboard. She opened the trunk but found that its tiny space would not come close to accommodating an eight-foot surfboard.

When she had just about given up, Jenna spotted a latch on top of the back seat. She pulled it, and half of the back seat flopped forward. Victory!

Through a combination of laying down the front and back seats, Jenna was able to get most of her board into the car, with only a foot of it sticking past the rear bumper. She carefully wrapped the back end of the surfboard in a towel and then used a bungee cord to hold down the trunk lid.

Her mom came out of the house and took one look at the packing job Jenna had performed and commented, "Good thing there are only two of us!"

Jenna couldn't agree more. She smiled and slid into the backseat behind her mother. She was glad that her mother's boyfriend was not around today.

The car started up, and slack key Hawaiian music flooded out over the radio.

Normally Jenna would have asked her mom to change the station to something with more of a rock 'n' roll sound, but today this was just fine. It sounded like the kind of music to go to the beach with—a soundtrack for a surfer girl.

When Jenna arrived at Pine Trees, she found the scene completely different than the day before.

Yesterday the place bustled with people and surfboards. Today the parking lot was almost empty and only a few clusters of people dotted the beach. The water was almost vacant of surfers.

She pulled her surfboard out of the car, actually said thank you to her mother, and slowly walked down the sandy trail to the beach.

Jenna was disappointed to see that none of the Hanalei girls were around. She laid the surfboard in the sand with the deck up and spread out her beach towel. Then she vigorously covered her pale body with sunblock. She didn't notice that the warm tropical sun had quickly melted the wax on her surfboard, turning the deck liquid with its slippery wax.

Jenna stared at the ocean and wondered how she should start. She secretly had hoped that someone—Malia, Bethany, or one of the other girls—would give her some pointers about surfing. But no one was there.

She would have to do it herself.

Jenna stood up and fumbled with the leash. She fastened it on her left ankle, which turned out to be the wrong leg, because she tried to stand on the surfboard and felt very awkward—like the leash might trip her. So she switched the leash to her right ankle.

Jenna picked up her surfboard, and the runny wax smeared along her arm. "Gross!" she said out loud.

Trudging toward the crashing waves, Jenna tried to remember what she had seen the day before so that she could imitate it.

She made a painful mistake. Rather than point the nose of her board toward the ocean, she put the board in the water sideways and tried to push it out to sea in that manner.

The first small wave to come rolling in picked up the surfboard and smacked it hard into Jenna's shins.

"Oww!" she cried, rubbing her legs.

When she recaptured her surfboard, Jenna pushed it a little way into the surf and then flopped on top of it. But the greasy sunblock that coated her body acted like butter on top of the now unwaxed board, and she slid off the side almost immediately. Over and over again she tried to find her balance in merely lying down on the board, but a bit of rolling whitewater kept sending her tumbling into the surf.

Jenna realized that this surfing sport was a lot harder than it looked and that she was going to need help.

Bethany and the girls trickled down the beach as they lugged their boards and gear, checking out the waves with the ease that comes from years of practice.

"The swells look a lot bigger today," Jasmine said. Bethany grinned at her, feeling the excitement of the challenge building inside.

"Yeah! No time to lose!" she declared as she quickly pulled the chunk of white surf wax from a pocket in her towel and scraped it across the surface of her board. A thick fresh coat of wax roughed up the wax that already covered the deck.

"There limps Malia!" Monica announced, looking up from working on her own board.

Sure enough, Malia was slowly hobbling down the trail, with a small knapsack on her back and a folding beach chair under her arm. She wore shorts and a T-shirt over her bathing suit.

"Malia, the surf has picked up," said Bethany excitedly.

"Yeah, I can see!" said Malia. "Looks like I'm watching today though."

"Yeah, too bad," Bethany said, encouraged to see her friend's smile. "I'm going to ride that far sand bar. It's cranking out perfect lefts!"

Bethany looked up to see a wet, pathetic figure stumble from the water. She was clearly exhausted and dragging behind her an old yellowed eight-foot surfboard.

It was Jenna.

Bethany quickly bent back over her board again and began to work on it so she wouldn't have to deal with the new girl. The other girls seemed to take her cue and continued to work on their boards in silence.

"Hi, Bethany!" Jenna said weakly.

"Uh, um, hi!" Bethany said with a sideways glance to Malia, who was now frowning. She looked away from Malia and tried to brush away the small pang of guilt that nudged at her heart.

Suddenly, the crack of a wave grabbed Bethany's and the other girls' attention. A huge set had just bombed into the bay.

"Whoa!" Bethany exclaimed.

"Um, Bethany," Jenna said, interrupting Bethany's thoughts of surfing, "I just got this surfboard and was...well, I'm kinda having a hard time figuring out how to do this, and I was wondering if you...especially since Malia is hurt...could give me a little help?"

Now it's true that the excitement of the magnificent waves rolling in had captured Bethany's attention. And it was also true that the presence of the restless girls in the pack behind her saying, "Come on, let's go!" put some pressure on. And it was true that this wet, pale girl was not part of her friendship circle or even on the radar screen of being a potential candidate to join the Hanalei Girls Surf Team. But what was most true was that Bethany didn't really *want* to get to know this new girl. She had already had a glimpse into what the girl was like and had decided she didn't care at all for what she saw.

So she gave Jenna a polite brush-off.

"Well, maybe later," Bethany said. "I'm gonna surf right now!" Then she added, trying to be helpful, "You'll probably find it a lot easier if you go up the beach and try to figure it out where the surf's not so big!"

Bethany saw the hopeful look on Jenna's face disappear as she quickly mumbled, "Okay, I understand," and turned away. She saw it—but pretended she didn't. Instead, Bethany slipped the piece of wax back into the pocket of her towel. When she looked up, Malia locked eyes with her, a disapproving frown deepening on her face.

"Grrrrr," growled Malia softly to Bethany. Nobody but Bethany heard with the crashing sound of waves in the background.

"Come on, Malia! Everyone has gotta learn on their own," Bethany said, knowing full well what Malia was saying to her. "*I'm going surfing!*" It sounded childish even to her own ears. She took off in a run to catch up with the other girls and paddled out into the lineup.

Bethany reveled in the sun-sparkled water, listening to the laughter of her friends. The waves were as awesome as she had imagined. It was one of those sweet days you wanted to remember forever. She was surfing well and strong, shredding wave after wave with skill and grace, *out-surfing* everyone else. But she wasn't having any fun.

She couldn't get Malia's growl out of her mind.

All at once Bethany felt the rush of feelings that she had tried to ignore over the last week flood over her heart. She felt guilty, selfish, and foolish. She knew she hadn't shown any mercy or understanding toward Jenna. She also knew that she had chosen to ignore the fact that her stable family life was a blessing that others might never get to taste.

Someone had asked for her help, and she had chosen to satisfy her own selfish desires instead. And now she was riding the best waves she had surfed in months, but she couldn't enjoy them.

Okay, God, Bethany prayed, cringing on the inside. *I'm sorry, I blew it.*

"I'm going back in!" Bethany suddenly announced as Monica paddled past her.

"What?" Monica glanced over, startled.

"I'll be back. I've got something to do," Bethany said with grim determination.

"Well, I hope you don't mind if I take your waves while you're gone," Monica called after her. But Bethany wasn't listening. She quickly caught the next wave and rode it all the way to the beach.

Unfastening the leash from her ankle, she trotted back to where Malia slumped in her beach chair.

"Where'd that kid go?" Bethany asked Malia, feeling a strange urgency come over her.

"You mean Jenna?" Malia said, shielding her eyes against the sun.

"Yeah," said Bethany. "I told her to go up the beach. The waves are smaller and easier to learn on next to the pier." Bethany squinted in that direction. "But I can't see her."

"I see somebody about to go into the water *down* the beach," Malia said, suddenly trying to stand. "And that's the *worst* place to go if you're a beginner."

Bethany turned and stared intently in the direction Malia had pointed.

"That's her!" Bethany exclaimed, and then she took off running as fast as her long legs could fly.

nine

Jenna had sat on the sand for a long time, trying to catch her breath from her recent attempt. Then a steely determination came over her. She would show those girls. She would learn to surf without any of their help. She would earn their respect and friendship by becoming as good a surfer as they were. Maybe better.

With determination, she had picked up her surfboard and started walking along the surf line. Bethany's tip for her was to head toward the gentle, small waves that were the learning ground for all the local kids.

Instead, she unknowingly headed toward a part of the beach with a whole different personality.

As Jenna came to the arch in the bay, she stopped and looked at the ocean. This looked like the perfect spot to paddle out. Waves broke on both sides, but here, right in front of her, was a fifty-foot patch of what looked to be calm water. She slipped the leash onto her ankle and waded into the surf.

The bottom was a mix of sand and reef. This bothered Jenna, but she reasoned that once she paddled out she could paddle back up the beach toward the sandy part of the break.

Lying down on her surfboard, she found that without any waves crashing into her she could balance herself with ease. Encouraged, she stroked out toward the horizon and found she was moving quickly.

This is easy, she thought.

But paddling used muscles she had never used before, and she was tiring quickly. Jenna pulled her arms out of the water and rested them on the edge of her board. To her astonishment, Jenna realized she was still moving. Without paddling she was being carried out toward the darker blue water.

She had paddled out in a rip.

Bethany, running down the beach, saw the red-headed girl lay her surfboard down in the deceptive calm of the riptide. She saw how quickly the girl and board were swept into deep water and felt her heart skip a beat.

By the time she got to the spot where Jenna had paddled out, Bethany was panting as she frantically scanned the waves for Jenna. *Please help me find her, God!*

Jenna felt a small trickle of fear wash over her as she realized she was being taken out much farther than she felt comfortable with. She tried to paddle her board back toward shore, but the current relentlessly carried her out to sea. Her weakening arms were almost useless now, and panic set in.

Suddenly, a huge wave seemed to loom out of nowhere. It crashed in front of the wide-eyed young girl. The explosion of whitewater that followed hurled Jenna off her surfboard and into a swirling, washing machine of foam and waves that twisted and turned her upside down, spinning her round and round as if she were a rag doll. Her arms and feet flailed, to no avail. The ocean was in control.

The wave loosened its grip, and she popped to the surface. In her desperation for air, she gasped and sucked down a gulp of saltwater as well. Coughing and sputtering, she looked around for help, but at the same terrible moment, Jenna realized something was pulling down on her leg, keeping her head from completely breaking free of the surface of the water.

She could see her surfboard lying flat on the face of the sea, ten feet away, but something was holding her. She couldn't move.

Under the water, Jenna's leash had wrapped around a coral reef head and, unknown to her, it was keeping her trapped in one location.

Jenna dog-paddled ferociously. Then in horror, she saw another wave loom up over her.

A wave of pure fear washed over Jenna. In a burst of energy she grappled with all her might against the force holding her down, and just as the wave cracked above her, she felt herself go free. Then came the tumbling and tossing darkness of the broken wave.

She had snapped the old leash and was free. But she was free without her lifeline. Her surfboard had washed away.

On the beach Bethany had finally spotted Jenna and quickly debated her options. The safest thing to do would be to sprint back to the lifeguard station and let the professionals handle this. But in Hawaii, with so many beaches, lifeguard stations are few and far between, placed in spots where large numbers of people gather.

Here in this corner of the bay, the nearest lifeguard was half a mile away. By the time they could respond, it would be too late.

Bethany's first impulse was to swim out to the girl, but she knew the danger of trying to rescue a panicking person. With only one arm to use, it could mean drowning for both of them.

But when the second wave hit Jenna and snapped her leash, a plan dropped into Bethany's head. Jenna's surfboard had been picked up by the onrushing wave and was sweeping toward the shore. Bethany was sure she could reach it and use it in the rescue.

She plunged into the surf, artfully dodging rocks and reef until she came to water deep enough to swim. With a powerful kick, honed to perfection in swim team, and stroking hard with one arm, Bethany cut through the water toward the bobbing surfboard.

Another wave was racing against Bethany for possession of the board. If the wave beat her to the goal, it could drag the surfboard farther away and out of reach or take it on to the rocks.

Bethany saw that the race would be close, and she pushed harder. Reaching the board at the same instant as Bethany, the wave grabbed the eight-foot chunk of foam and wrenched it from her grasp.

As it sailed by, Bethany felt the remnants of the leash slide past her hand. She closed her fist and snagged it. Quickly pulling the surfboard toward her, Bethany scrambled onto it with ease.

Now powerfully stroking with one strong arm, she plowed into the frothing white water, gripping hard to the edge of the surfboard to keep it from being wrenched from her hands as she paddled toward the bobbing red head in the distance.

Jenna had gone into full panic mode, coughing up water. She was disoriented by having been spun around by the powerful wave surge. She was tired and weak, her dog paddling only barely keeping her buoying above water. Fear gave way to a desperate automatic struggle to survive—a struggle that the next set wave rising on the horizon could end.

The horrible knowledge that she could die swept through her mind. She had almost given into the inevitability of it when she remembered her father's words to her, *"God has plans for you — a future for you . . . full of hope."*

Jenna saw the whitewater explode thirty feet in front of her. She knew that when it rolled over her, she would not have the strength to fight anymore.

Suddenly, the yellowing nose of her old surfboard floated into view. At the same time she felt a strong arm pull her onto the deck.

"Hold on tight!" demanded Bethany.

The wave was almost on top of the two girls.

Bethany covered Jenna with much of her body as she shifted the weight of both of their bodies to maneuver the board in the direction of the shore.

The whitewater hit them with a jolt. Bethany held on to Jenna with her arm and clasped the back rails of the surfboard between her knees to keep the pair from washing off.

With the first shock of the powerful water, the surfboard launched out in front of the rolling wave, and Jenna felt herself being propelled shoreward at an incredible speed.

She heard Bethany's soothing voice from behind saying, "We're fine, we're fine, we're almost there."

Within moments, sand appeared under the board, and Bethany slid off the back into waist-deep water and pushed Jenna along.

A small wave came rushing from behind and picked up the surfboard in its path. Bethany turned loose, and Jenna felt herself racing toward the beach.

"Stand up!" Bethany shouted.

As tired and weak as she was, the encouraging voice shot something extra into her, and Jenna pushed herself up on the board, standing in a wide stinkbug-looking stance.

She rode all the way to the beach with the voice of Bethany cheering behind her.

As they walked along the beach, Bethany carried the exhausted girl's surfboard.

"Thank you," Jenna said quietly. "I was just about to give up."

"Well, you can't do that," Bethany said kindly. "And you can't give up on surfing, either."

Bethany stopped walking for a moment and looked Jenna straight in the eye. "Jenna, I'm really sorry about being so cold and selfish when you first asked for help learning to surf. God is still working on me. In fact, he was working on me big time after you walked away, which is how I ended up being where you were a few minutes ago."

"What do you mean, God is still working on you?" asked Jenna.

"It's kind of like a voice that whispers to you, and you know it's not your own thoughts," Bethany explained shyly.

"I think I've heard something like that voice," Jenna said with a note of amazement. They looked at each other and smiled.

For the rest of the walk back to where Malia waited, Bethany explained to Jenna about her relationship with Jesus Christ and how he wants to be invited into a relationship with everyone and to grow inside of them. She explained to her about how God had given her strength to conquer her fears after the shark attack and how he was beside her as she struggled to relearn to surf.

What Bethany said felt right to Jenna. Jenna could remember things her dad had said to her years ago about God—that God was "her rock." Jenna felt that God was probably talking to her too ... through her memories of her dad.

"I thought you were just strong and determined," Jenna said, glancing over at Bethany.

"Not strong and determined enough to do it without God's help," said Bethany. "Everybody, sooner or later, finds themselves getting washed around in life, kind of like you did out there. Without him, we drown!"

"It's a lot to think about," Jenna said. "But it kind of makes sense."

"Yeah, well, take it in slowly," said Bethany. "It's like surfing; you learn an awful lot just by trying and failing."

"Well, I won't have any trouble with that part," Jenna said wryly, and they both laughed.

Malia, who had helplessly watched the drama unfold, quickly hobbled down the beach to meet the pair.

"Jenna! That's *down* the beach, not *up* the beach! It's only for experts down there!"

"Yeah, I found that out," said Jenna.

"Why don't you rest a while and get something to eat," said Bethany. "My ice chest is the blue one over there. My mom always puts in extra stuff, so help yourself!"

"Thanks," said Jenna.

"I'm going surfing, but when I come back in, I promise, I'll give you surf lessons!" said Bethany.

"I think that might be a good idea," Jenna said with a grin.

"We all need lessons from time to time," Bethany said, but she was looking at Malia, smiling.

"See ya in a bit!" she said after a moment.

With that, she jogged down to the edge of the ocean and plunged in.

ten

A cooling breeze lifted the curtains in Jenna's room. Outside her window, ginger plants were in bloom, and the breeze brought their delicate sweet smell in with it.

On the wall, Jenna had pinned pictures of waves next to pictures of horses in full gallop. She was a child of the ocean now too, but more important, she was also a child of God.

Jenna glanced up from the New Testament that she had been reading while lying on her bed, and she smiled—a smile that she felt deep in her heart.

It had been six months since Bethany had pulled her in from the surf, and Jenna would be the first to admit, it hadn't always been easy. But it had been exciting *and* adventurous.

She had worked hard to get the fundamentals of surfing down pat. And with encouragement from Bethany, Malia, and the other girls of the Hanalei Surf Team, she had enrolled in swimming lessons at the neighborhood pool.

"We aren't coming out to rescue you again if your leash breaks," they had told her. "You're gonna have to swim yourself outta those problems."

While not yet tackling the bigger, more dangerous waves, Jenna felt right at home on the smaller, zippy waves.

The Hanalei girls had, for the most part, been gracious and warm toward her. Monica was less than thrilled with her entry into the friendship circle and still kept a cool distance from her. But Bethany, Malia, and the rest of the girls had made Jenna a welcomed guest at their spot at the beach anytime she showed up.

And Jenna had discovered something else in her journey around the island: there were actual *cowboys* living in Hawaii! Not much different than those she had known in Arizona. Thanks to her new friend from the garage sale, she learned that the *paniolo*, or Hawaiian cowboy, is an old and revered part of the island culture.

Because there were stables nearby where visitors would take horseback rides into the Kauai backcountry, Jenna was able to find an after-school job grooming and caring for horses. She still didn't own one outright, but the owners kindly allowed her to saddle and ride one of her favorites whenever possible.

But the biggest change in Jenna's life was that she had discovered firsthand what it meant to know Jesus Christ as Lord and Savior.

At first she had been cautious, even a bit skeptical about the whole God thing. But so many of the girls she had met seemed to talk about God in an easy, relaxed, and natural way, as if it were the most obvious and common thing to talk to him, be guided by him, and live for him.

These girls (and not a few guys) were not weird, sheltered church kids. They were attractive, normal, fun-loving teenagers who seemed to find excitement, energy, and fun without the typical mix of sex, alcohol, or drugs.

Jenna was fascinated, and for a time she merely watched and listened. And even though Sarah Hill had offered to pick her up for youth group or for church on Sunday, she resisted. As always, she wanted to find her way on her own.

Thankfully, it didn't take another near-death moment for her to see the truth. It just seemed to grow in her day by day until one day, she finally accepted Sarah's invitation and started attending youth group meetings, and then occasionally, the big tent church.

What Sarah taught made good sense to her. Jenna asked if it might be possible to get a Bible, and later that evening Sarah dropped off a brand-new and very easy-to-read copy of the New Testament.

Somewhere in the middle of her reading that night, Jenna had put down the Bible and said a few simple words to God. She sensed that she had crossed a line. That there was something real and powerful going on, and it seemed to be the turning point in her life. She had become a believer in Christ.

Her mom was skeptical about the new faith thing, but Jenna never wavered. And not long after she had made the decision to follow Jesus, she also made another very important step. She apologized to her mom for all the times that she had hurt her. Even though it was hard for them to see eye to eye sometimes, she knew in her heart she needed to make an effort to be nicer to her mom.

Because it mattered to God...and her mom too.

Not long after she apologized, her mom had actually agreed to go to church with Jenna when she could make it.

Jenna heard the gravel driveway crunch under the tires of a car. She jumped from her bed, grabbed a small backpack and ice chest, which sat in the hallway, and burst through the door.

Sarah's car, roof rack stacked high with surfboards, stopped in front of her house.

"Come on, slowpoke, let's go!" called someone from inside the car.

Jenna tossed her gear in the back end of Sarah's car and then ran back onto the porch. She produced a small surfboard wrapped in a striped red board bag.

"Wow! New board?" one of the girls asked.

"New used board," Jenna said with a grin. "Bethany gave it to me ... said she outgrew it."

"It's a lot shorter than your old eight-footer," said Sarah. "Can you ride it?"

"We'll find out soon enough!"

Just then the postal carrier pulled up and stuck a wad of mail into the mailbox.

"Hold on a second," Jenna said to Sarah as she jumped out of the car to check the mail.

Rummaging through the mailbox, she pulled out a large colorful postcard and ran back to the car.

"Whatcha get?" asked Sarah.

"It's a postcard from Bethany," Jenna said.

"Where is she now?" asked one of the girls, with just a hint of jealousy in her voice.

"This postcard is from Australia," said Jenna.

"That Bethany is sooooo lucky," said Malia from the front seat. "I wish I could travel around the world like she does."

"This time of year, the water is pretty cold down under," reminded Sarah. "I'm sure Bethany has to wear a wetsuit and booties."

"Ugh, I hate cold water! She can have it," one of the girls responded.

"She says here that she and her family are going to Samoa after they leave Australia. Where's Samoa?" Jenna asked.

"It's somewhere south of us," Malia said.

It took over an hour of driving to get to their spot. The winter swells that normally give surf to the Hanalei side of the island were starting to diminish, and the swells coming from the southern hemisphere were beginning to show up on the other side of the island.

Sarah had offered to take her crew on a "surfari" to the south side of the island to grab the new south swell hitting those shores.

Eventually, the girls stood on the coarse sand in front of a surf spot called the Waiohai. This place was all reef bottom and sharp as well. Surfing this spot would have been unthinkable for Jenna a few months before, but today she confidently looked at the crisp lefts without a speck of fear.

Tourists from the nearby hotel clogged just about every available space on the sand, but the girls managed to find an open spot where they could drop their ice chests and towels.

After waxing up their boards, they stood on the edge of the water together, looking at the break in the distance.

"Anyone care to offer up a prayer before we go?" asked Sarah.

"I will," Jenna said without hesitation.

In an Australian hotel room Bethany rubbed a sore calf muscle as a chilly rain soaked the patio furniture outside. She had not done as well as she had hoped in her contest heat, but she knew that this was just one competition among many and that she would have more chances to move up in the ratings.

The cold water always played havoc with her calf muscles if she didn't stretch extra before surfing, and now she was paying the price.

On the dresser, her mom had left the travel brochures for the surf camp in Samoa that they would be heading to after Australia. Bethany felt the excitement of the trip warm her in spite of the weather. This would be a family vacation—a surfing family vacation to be exact. No contests, no photo shoots, no people looking for autographs. Just two weeks hidden away at a remote beach camp.

And even better, the camp held only twelve surfers. With the five Hamiltons, that left only seven other surfers at the camp to deal with.

"This oughta be heaven," Bethany whispered.

Then she picked up a letter that was at the top of their mail stack and saw that it was from Jenna. She opened the letter and took out a single sheet of stationery.

Dear Bethany,

> *You'll never guess what I did when I was reading the New Testament the other afternoon! I accepted Jesus as my Savior! Aren't you excited?*

*It's only been a few days, but I feel
so different. Like Jesus is right there,
next to me. It's so awesome.*

*I'm learning more all the time
about surfing and about God. Thanks
again for giving me your board—I
rode on it the other day, and it's pretty
sweet.*

*I hope you're having a cool time
surfing down under.*

Love,
Jenna

Bethany folded the letter and gently wiped a
tear from her eye. Her mom's words as she lay in
that hospital room a lifetime ago came back to her.

*What an awesome opportunity you've
been given! To share your faith with so many
people—people you might never have met if this
hadn't happened.*

Bethany hadn't really understood those words
at the time—and had actually wondered how she
could help someone else when she was still learning how to help herself.

Thank you for Jenna, Lord, Bethany prayed.
*Thank you for teaching me that when we help oth-
ers, we help ourselves grow closer to you.*

Bethany grinned, remembering Sarah's words:
"*God may put a treasure in your path that you*

don't recognize. Sometimes the treasure is crusty on the surface, but after you wash off the dirt, you find the real value there."

Burned

a novel

CHECK OUT
this excerpt
from book two in the
Soul Surfer Series.

written by Rick Bundschuh
inspired by Bethany Hamilton

 *one*

Bethany felt like she had stepped into another world—or *something* like that.

Still groggy from the plane trip from Australia, she blinked a couple of times and pulled her iPod headset down around her neck as she glanced around the busy little airport. Samoa didn't seem like the Treasure Island that her mom was so into talking about lately—but it did kind of feel like another world.

A world of giants.

Giants that wore knee-length wraparound skirts—or *lavalavas* as her mom called them. She watched the group of men as they passed her by with their suitcases and grinned to herself. *Bet no one would mistake them for girls!* She glanced at Noah as he fell into step beside her.

"*Big* people, huh?"

"I wouldn't want to play rugby against any of these guys," Noah admitted.

"You wouldn't last playing rugby against any of the *girls!*" Tim said, eyeing Noah's thin frame with a sly grin.

"I don't know—the girls are really pretty," Bethany laughed. "Might be worth the pain." Her attention was suddenly drawn to the group ahead of them. *Had to be surfers*, she thought, eyeing the three young guys with their sun-bleached hair and trademark broad shoulders. The youngest turned and said something to one of the older boys. Bethany guessed him to be close to her age. He had long wavy hair and his nose and cheeks were speckled from constant peeling. The bright red shirt he was wearing had the logo of a California surfboard company on it.

Surfers—I knew it! Bethany thought smugly.

"At least *I'm* not crazy enough to get a tattoo," Noah said as he shifted the board bag to his other shoulder. Bethany glanced back at him, momentarily confused.

"Tattoo?" She looked between her brothers and frowned. That's what she got for sleeping on the plane; she always missed the good stuff.

"*Samoan* tattoo," Tim nodded excitedly. "They're awesome; a lot of geometric design. Really tribal."

Bethany made a face. "Only thing I want on my skin is some sun."

"You're not getting anything tattooed, Tim," Bethany's dad said dryly from somewhere behind them as their mom laughed.

Tim grinned. "Or how about a *Maori* tattoo— you know, the big ones that cover your face?"

"Might be an improvement, Dad," Noah interjected.

"Don't give him any ideas," Bethany's mom said exasperatedly, and they all laughed as they headed for customs.

Other than the surfboards, the Hamiltons traveled light; each had a carry-on with shorts, bathing suits, T-shirts, and one set of "going to dinner clothes." They moved quickly through the line and into the night.

Outside, the warm humid air blew around Bethany, reminding her of home. She turned her face toward the star-spattered sky. Actually it *was* home, having her family with her. Even though it was almost midnight, she felt the excitement of being in a new place and couldn't help wondering what kind of waves she would catch this trip.

When she looked down again, she noticed a huge, dark-skinned man leaning against the van parked at the curb. He was wearing a flowered aloha shirt, a lavalava, and a pair of well-worn rubber slippers.

She saw his eyes take in their surfboard bags, and he began to wave wildly, charging over to grab the heavier of the loads.

"*Talafoa*! My name is Tagiilima," he said, extending a large palm to Tom, Bethany's dad. "You Hamiltons?"

Bethany's dad nodded, and Tagiilima vigorously shook his hand—along with the rest of his body.

Soul Surfer Series

Body and Soul

A Girl's Guide to a Fit, Fun and Fabulous Life

Bethany Hamilton
with Dustin Dillberg

Bethany Hamilton has become a fitness expert by virtue of being a professional athlete who has excelled—and she's done it while overcoming incredible challenges. In *Body & Soul*, a total wellness book for girls ages 8 and up, Bethany shares some of her own experiences while helping young girls gain confidence and develop a pattern of healthy living starting at a young age. In addition to workouts and recipes, Bethany also shares her unstoppable faith and emphasizes how spiritual health is just as important as physical health.

Includes:

- Workouts specially developed for young girls by Bethany's personal trainer
- Recipes and information on healthy eating based on "Bethany's food pyramid," which follows the Mediterranean diet
- Advice on deepening your spiritual health and total body wellness

Available in stores and online!

Ask Bethany, Updated Edition

Bethany Hamilton
with Doris Rikkers

From Bethany Hamilton's fan letters come these honest, sometimes gut-wrenching questions. Some questions you may have asked about yourself at some time. Bethany's sincere answers reflect her faith, and with some of her favorite Scripture verses, her answers will inspire you, let you into Bethany's heart, and possibly help you with some of your own life questions.

Rise Above, Updated Edition

A 90-Day Devotional

Bethany Hamilton
with Doris Rikkers

Rise Above is a 90-day devotional from surfing star Bethany Hamilton where she shares with young girls her courage and enthusiasm for God, inspiring them to face life head on and stand strong in their faith.

Available in stores and online!

Soul Surfer Series

Clash

Rick Bundschuh, Inspired by Bethany Hamilton

Book one in the Soul Surfer Series

Burned

Rick Bundschuh, Inspired by Bethany Hamilton

Book two in the Soul Surfer Series

Storm

Rick Bundschuh, Inspired by Bethany Hamilton

Book three in the Soul Surfer Series

Crunch

Rick Bundschuh, Inspired by Bethany Hamilton

Book four in the Soul Surfer Series

Available in stores and online!